UNCERTAIN SUMMER

Praise for *Uncertain Summer*

"Readers with a hunger for outdoor adventure and the mysteries of cryptozoology will love joining Everdil's unstoppable team." —Kelly Milner Halls, author, *In Search of Sasquatch*

"While Everdil pulls and pushes her way through evolving relationships ..., the ongoing search moves toward a climax as harrowing and, nearly, tragic as it is revelatory." —*Kirkus Reviews*

"For every kid who has ever dreamed of doing something big, who has mourned friendships past, who has known with all their heart that they can make a difference ... *Uncertain Summer* is an absolute must!" —P.J. Hoover, author, *Tut: The Story of My Immortal Life*

"One thing is certain, *Uncertain Summer* is an action packed adventure you don't want to miss!" —Margie Longoria, librarian, book blogger, *Margie's Must Reads*

Praise for Jessica Lee Anderson's *Trudy*

"This quiet story is well paced, flowing through very short chapters. It offers a matter-of-fact, yet unique look at one family's changing dynamics." —*School Library Journal*

"By portraying Trudy's relationship with her aging and ill father, author Jessica Lee Anderson offers a tender and interesting twist on the traditional awkward-middle-school experience ..." —*Children's Literature*

Praise for Jessica Lee Anderson's *Border Crossing*

"A fast read, this book will provoke discussion and, perhaps, further research." —*Booklist*

"The poignant story of Manz, a 15-year-old boy trying to cope with a dysfunctional relationship with his alcoholic mother and the humming noises, whispering voices and scary visions that only he perceives." —*Kirkus Reviews*

"This taut coming of age novel explores mental illness and border issues in an honest and clear voice." —*Boys Read*

Praise for Jessica Lee Anderson's *Calli*

2013 Rainbow List Final Nomination

YALSA's Readers' Choice Booklist Nomination

"Calli's household consists of two moms, a devious foster sister, and a whole boatload of deceptions, double crosses and heart-ache. Here is a tale about telling the truth, about forgiveness, and about making things right, especially for yourself." —Kathi Appelt, author of *The Underneath and Keeper*

"[The] first-person, present-tense narration wrings emotion at every opportunity." —*Kirkus Reviews*

"This coming-of-age story from Austin writer Jessica Lee Anderson is finely wrought, with emotional twists that will absorb your teen reader." —*Austin American Statesman*

UNCERTAIN SUMMER

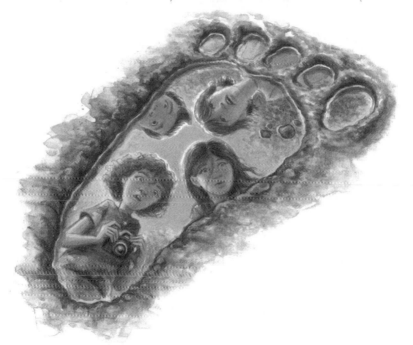

JESSICA LEE ANDERSON

ILLUSTRATIONS BY JEFF CROSBY

CBAY Books
Dallas, TX

Uncertain Summer

Cover design and illustrations by Jeff Crosby.
jeffcrosbyillustration.com

CBAY Books
PO Box 670296
Dallas, TX 75367

Children's Brains are Yummy Books
Dallas, Texas
www.cbaybooks.com

ISBN: 978-1-944821-24-1
eBook ISBN: 978-1-944821-25-8
Kindle ISBN: 978-1-944821-26-5
PDF ISBN: 978-1-944821-27-2

To Ava—my love for you is a billion times bigger than Bigfoot

Dear Cryptic Cryptids Productions,

Bigfoot exists. I'm convinced I saw the creature firsthand, and I've had some REALLY unusual experiences. People probably tell you stories like this all the time, and I bet a lot of them are lying or are crazy. I promise you I'm not lying, and I'm not crazy, though I admit I've had a few dishonest moments and felt like I was losing my mind at times. I know I'm not following the rules exactly, but I hope you'll still consider this submission. You have no idea how much it means to me, my family, and even to Bigfoot.

I know you're busy with the contest and all, but can you call as soon as you get this?

Love,
Everdil Jackson

My twelfth birthday arrived with more surprises than I expected.

To prepare for my big day, I'd helped Mama and Emmett plan a gourmet dinner party menu of fried gator bites, smoked salmon deviled eggs, bacon-wrapped scallops, and key lime pie.

What a waste of time.

I sent out the invitations to all of my friends, well except for Tim since things hadn't been right between us since the hand incident, and the "no" responses came rolling in since most everyone I knew was out of town for summer break. Shawna, my former best friend, didn't even bother with a reply.

I scrapped the gourmet dinner idea because deep down I knew we couldn't really afford it anyway and asked for a pizza party with the family instead. At least a pizza party meant more time at the lake for my favorite birthday tradition: the boat ride.

As Papa called in the pizza order, he rifled through a nearby stack of papers. His face paled to the color of the cream cheese frosting Emmett was whipping up. "One extra-large pepperoni," he said, right as Mama tried to take the bill from him. Papa's grip was firm. "Thank you," he added before hanging up. He definitely wasn't thanking Mama.

"I can explain," she said.

Papa raised an eyebrow as well as his voice. "Look at these charges. We owe more than I made all of last month."

"The kids needed a few things, and so did I," Mama said, glancing at the heavy-duty blender she'd bought after watching a FoodieLand infomercial. I'm no cook like her or Emmett, but even I wanted to pulverize, dice, and whirl fruits and vegetables like magic.

"How can I become a decent chef if I don't have the proper tools?" Mom asked.

Papa sighed. "I know, Macy. It's just that I have a surprise and—"

"Other than our gift?" Mama said in a low voice, but not so low I couldn't hear her.

They argued until Papa looked over at me sitting on the couch. I pretended like I was engrossed in the act of flipping through TV stations. As if guided by fate, I randomly changed the station to Cryptic Cryptid Productions and found out about this contest—a one million dollar reward for an unaltered, authenticated picture or video of Bigfoot. The small print on the screen revealed that the production company was not responsible for any related attacks or injuries, and the deadline was June 15. Only ten days away.

Someone said something, but thoughts of Bigfoot and a million dollars overloaded my brain, and it didn't register. With that much money, life would be easier for my entire family. If I won, maybe next year I could have that gourmet birthday dinner, and all my friends would come.

A Bigfoot picture had to be next to impossible, not to mention dangerous, but people I actually knew had reported sightings and survived without an attack, so I wasn't scared.

Our small town of Uncertain is no stranger to Bigfoot. It even has a road named after the beast, and there's a lodge for tourists called Bigfoot Retreat with a mascot staked out front, a black wooden Bigfoot cutout with a golden bow tie dangling around its thick neck. Along with Shawna and Tim, Emmett and I used to play Bigfoot hunting games, and maybe, just maybe—

"Earth to Everdil!" Emmett yelled from the kitchen, and then he launched something small and shiny at my head.

Only a low wall separated the short distance from the kitchen to the living room, and I failed to duck down fast enough. *WHAP!* The thing hit me behind my ear and got caught up in my web of brown frizzy curls. It was a metal decorating tip complete with clumps of sticky frosting. Gross.

Emmett hid behind a brand new wooden kitchen cart in anticipation of me retaliating. I balled my hand around the decorating tip, but I resisted the temptation to launch it at him. The frosting warmed in my hand, oozing into the folds of my palm. I'd pay him back when he let his guard down.

My grandfather chuckled as he finished taking his boots off in the entryway. I'd been so caught up in my daydream after my parents' argument that I hadn't realized he'd arrived. Now, thanks to Emmett's rudeness, I was back in the real world. "Hey, Gramps."

"Happy birthday, Everdil Pickle," Gramps said.

"Everdil Pickle Breath," Emmett added. I pretended not to hear him.

Gramps walked over to give me one of his legendary squeeze hugs. I made sure not to get frosting on his favorite flannel shirt that he wore year round, even in the Texas summer heat.

"I'd better go pick up the pizza," Papa said, grabbing his truck keys from the table in the front entryway with so much force that they skidded across the floor when he dropped them. He cursed under his breath as he picked them up.

"You okay, Raleigh?" Gramps asked and then lowered his voice. "Did the bank call again?"

Papa shook his head no and whispered, "We'll talk about it later."

I don't think Mama and Emmett overheard them from the kitchen, but Gramps must've known I had because after Papa left, he sat next to me on the couch and nudged me with his elbow. "Nothing to worry about. Today should be all about celebrating you. And believe me, there are plenty of surprises in store."

Again with the surprise talk.

Gramps started to say something else, but a loud announcer from Cryptic Cryptid Productions interviewed a team of hunters from California outfitted like soldiers. "We're determined to solve the mystery of Bigfoot once and for all. The monetary prize is just frosting on the cake," one of the hunters said.

I laughed and tasted the sticky sweet frosting on my hand.

"Those hunters might actually stand a chance if they came to Uncertain, not that I'd tip them off," Gramps said and then laughed at his own joke.

The thought of discovering Bigfoot in our town sped my pulse up.

Gramps launched into a story I hadn't heard him tell in over a year, not since Gram had a heart attack and "graduated to Heaven" as Gramps liked to say.

"Gram and I had just gone on our first date at the dance hall," Gramps said and then stopped to clear his throat before continuing. "I was driving her home on Marshall Loop when we heard a loud scream, sort of noise like a bear might make. I slammed on the brakes when I spotted an enormous creature off to the side of the road. It stood upright and was larger than any bear I'd ever seen. Even if I'd carried a gun on me, there's no way I could've shot it 'cause its eyes were so humanlike. I parked the car in the middle of the road, and we watched that thing hop a fence."

Gramps acted out the last part of the story with wild hand gestures. Emmett moved in closer to the living room to eavesdrop.

I hurled the decorating tip back at him now, but his reflexes were Superman-quick. He dodged the tip, and it clanked against the cabinet before sliding across the kitchen floor.

Mama joined us in the living room after pouring herself a cup of iced tea. She sighed one of those sighs that could mean anything. "Oh, Dad, you're a natural storyteller, just like Raleigh. You should take him up on the offer to give tours."

Gramps swallowed hard. "I'm telling the truth about Bigfoot, not fiction."

Mama sighed again.

"Tim's dad recently heard a similar report," Emmett said after a moment of silence. Tim's dad, Mr. Nash, happened to be a well-respected park ranger at Caddo Lake State Park with a wild Bigfoot story of his own.

"And look at Swamp Sam," I added, referring to Papa's boss at the marina.

"Swamp Sam isn't the best example," Emmett said.

My brother made a good point. Swamp Sam (no one seemed to know his real name) believed Bigfoot had visited him at the cabin a few times and sent him subliminal messages about an upcoming apocalypse. He once spent a month wearing a cowboy hat lined with tinfoil so the government couldn't track him … before he got admitted to the hospital.

"I wish I could go back in time to see Bigfoot with Gram again," Gramps said, and his voice broke as he reached into his pocket. When he pulled out a folded tissue, I thought he was about to dab his eyes. Then I saw a familiar looking shiny pearl strung on a thin gold chain nestled in his hand. "Your grandmother would've wanted you to have this, Everdil."

I was too stunned to say anything. I knew the whole story of the necklace— how my grandfather had gone looking for sunken treasure on Caddo Lake when he was young though the only thing he found was a mussel with this pearl inside. Gramps used the necklace to propose to Gram instead of an engagement ring.

I looked over at Mama to see her reaction. Really, the necklace should belong to her not me, considering she's his daughter. It's like Mama read my mind. "Gram really did want you to have this. She said so the day you were born. Your grandfather talked to me beforehand, and we both agree you're mature enough to take proper care of it now that you're twelve."

Gramps smiled and then helped me put the necklace on. "Gram said the pearl reminded her that we were rich even if we were always broke," he said. "We were rich in love, health, friends, and family—the important stuff, though you're probably too young to realize this."

Mama sniffled, and I wasn't sure what to say other than a heartfelt, "Thank you."

The necklace felt so light on my neck that I reached for the pearl to make sure it was still there. The gem wasn't much bigger than my fingertip.

The special gift felt like a good omen.

2

While the pizza was piping hot, Papa had cooled off some by the time he got home.

"Sorry about earlier," he said to no one in particular. "Tonight should be about celebrating Everdil, and I've got something major in store."

Mama arched her eyebrows up like she didn't have a clue what he was talking about, but right as she opened her mouth to say something, Papa cut her off by announcing, "Let's eat!"

As we took our seats, I tilted my chin toward the ceiling for Papa to notice the jewelry, but he got the wrong idea instead. "Good thinking, Everdil. We can't forget to say grace." Papa rushed through a prayer before my hands fully clasped together. He followed that up by flinging paper plates at us like they were Frisbees.

I snickered when Emmett's plate hit his Adam's apple. So much for his Superman reflexes. Mama gave Papa the evil eye when a plate glided onto her lap. Only Gramps was quick enough to catch his—one handed no less. Mine slid onto the floor, and when I went to pick it up, I found the decorating tip. I thought about sliding it into Emmett's shoe but brought it to the sink instead. If it got ruined, we'd likely need to buy a whole new set of decorating tips and that might lead to another argument.

The financial stuff and the tension had shrunk my appetite some, but it returned full force when Gramps lifted the cardboard box open. The smell of freshly baked pizza dough, spicy sauce, pepperoni, and mozzarella rushed out. Yum!

"You're not going to let Everdil drive the boat tonight, are you?" Emmett asked with his mouth full. He must've been dwelling on the surprises in store for tonight, too. My brother sounded kind of jealous if you ask me.

"Perhaps," Papa said. From the way he scratched the stubble on his chin, I could tell the thought had just now occurred to him.

"She should have to wait another year," Emmett said. Papa had let him drive the boat when he'd turned thirteen, and he obviously didn't think I should have the same privileges.

"Let's wait and see," Mama said.

I wasn't ready to let it go yet. "C'mon, Papa, give me a hint? Please?"

He started talking with bits of tomato sauce wedged in his front tooth. "A big opportunity—a huge opportunity—came my way." He turned to Mama as he made a correction. "*Our* way."

"What's that supposed to mean, Raleigh?"

"You'll see soon," Papa said, avoiding her intense stare. He turned toward Emmett instead. "That cake sure looks delicious."

Changing the subject was a smart idea, and I followed his lead. "Look, Papa," I said, pointing to the necklace.

He actually noticed it this time. "It's beautiful, Everdil, just like you."

My cheeks grew warm and even warmer when Gramps said, "I couldn't agree more." He'd been especially quiet throughout dinner, and I thought it might've been because he was missing Gram so much.

Gram had a way of putting everyone at ease, no matter what, and she loved making people laugh. Just like Mama watched a whole lot of FoodieLand, Gram had been addicted to a station called Laugh Box. Don't ask me how, but she and Gramps had gotten into telling Chuck Norris "facts"—stuff like how Chuck Norris never reads a book, he just stares at the pages and demands information instead.

I missed her like crazy.

"Thanks again, Gramps, I love it," I said, "and Papa's right, Emmett. The cake looks delicious."

My brother beamed ... or was that a suspicious glint in his eyes?

"Emmett, you've really outdone yourself this time," Mama said. She went on and on about his "culinary aptitude" like she has a tendency to do. She even has a pet cooking nickname for him—her precious "sous chef."

In this case, he wasn't a mere assistant, though. Emmett was the sole creator of a double-decker red velvet cake with extra thick cream cheese frosting. He'd piped the sides of the cake with the most delicate of roses. You would never guess that this same kid was a renowned running back on the school football team. At least legendary for a super small town football team.

Emmett excused himself from the table to grab the cake, and Mama helped him light the candles, only ten because that's all we had in stock. My brother insisted he should be the one to carry the glowing cake over to the table but took his ever-loving time about it. Two of the candles blew out before my family finished singing the birthday song. I almost expected some kind of trick as I huffed out the candles, but they didn't sparkle or re-light or anything else. Even though I knew better given the reality, I made a wish that I'd somehow, someway, win the million dollar Bigfoot contest.

I laughed to myself because of how childish and crazy that sounded. Emmett gave me a funny look as he carved the cake. He didn't press me about it, though, and served me an extra-large slice.

"I hope you like it," he said right as I took a big mouthful.

The frosting was so sugary it tickled my tongue, but as I bit into the red, fluffy cake, a bitter taste assaulted my taste buds. The tickly tongue feeling morphed into more of a frothy sensation. I looked down at my piece of cake and saw a big white clump of powder. I spat it out. Emmett had sabotaged my delicious looking present!

All Emmett's pranks piled up in my mind—how he once

wrote on my forehead with permanent marker while I slept, the time he dipped my toothbrush in soft soap before putting it back in the cup, and when he poured liquid bubbles into my nearly empty can of soda. Not to mention the name calling. So many of my birthday plans had changed, and now my cake was ruined, too. That was it. Time for frosting comeuppance!

I smashed my piece into Emmett's face.

Frosting wedged up his nose and bits of red cake plopped down on his favorite t-shirt, leaving a spot of grease on the yellow fabric. With wide eyes, my brother wiped his face with a napkin, but then his expression darkened. "You're an awful sister, and you ruin everything!" He rushed out of the room and slammed his door so loud that it echoed down the hall.

Mama had to spit her bite of cake in a napkin before she could properly fuss at me. "Everdil Lynn Jackson, you should be ashamed of yourself!"

Papa joined in the yell-at-Everdil-a-thon, but Gramps stayed out of it. His look of disappointment was worse than my parent's angry words, though. I swear the gold chain burned around my neck like a ring of shame. "I'm sorry."

"You better go tell Emmett you're sorry instead," Mama said. "It's an honest baker's mistake not to sift the baking soda."

Emmett had it coming to him, but I felt worse knowing he might not have ruined the cake on purpose.

"Your mother's right, Everdil. You owe your brother an apology," Papa said, his voice so stern I shriveled in my seat.

I trudged my way to Emmett's room wishing for some kind of life rewind button. When I recorded one of Mama's FoodieLand auditions so she might become a star chef instead of a short order cook at the Uncertain Café, I could hit stop and do another take. There was no easy out for me here—I swallowed my pride and asked for forgiveness.

As much as I wanted another go at things, Emmett wasn't hearing any of my requests for forgiveness. "Sorry, Emmett. I didn't mean to." Well, technically, I did mean to smash the cake in his face, but I could've paid him back in a much less obvious way.

"Go away, Everdil!"

A moment later I heard a scraping sound. He must've been moving his furniture to keep me out.

"Be that way," I said, "but I really am sorry."

Emmett still refused to come out of his room. Papa knocked on his door. "C'mon, son, I want you to join us tonight."

When Emmett continued to ignore him, Papa searched for his toolkit to unhinge the door, but Mama talked him out of it. "The boy needs some alone time. Don't you remember what it's like to be thirteen?" she asked him.

Papa must've, because he let Emmett be.

I hadn't gotten grounded so the least I could do was clean up the kitchen to return to my parents' good graces. I threw out all of the greasy paper plates and the rest of the trash, but I didn't have the heart to chuck the remaining cake. I put the cake lid back over the dish. The frosting was salvageable, right?

"Emmett will come around," Gramps said as he refilled his glass of sweet tea. "Gram and I had our fair share of spats, but as Chuck Norris would say, that's just part of being a family."

Gramps was off—this was no Chuck Norris fact, but I didn't have the heart to correct him. "I guess."

Once all traces of grease disappeared from the kitchen table and I washed my hands, Mama and Papa presented me with a rectangular box wrapped in shiny pink paper. "We should wait to give this to you after the stunt you pulled, but it *is* your birthday, and this will be useful for all of us," Mama said. Maybe she'd been paying attention to how Emmett constantly provoked me after all.

I tore into the cotton candy pink paper. I couldn't believe it. My parents had bought me a digital camera with fancy recording features.

"Now you have better equipment to direct auditions with!" Mama said. She'd been blaming our camcorder's lack of video quality as the reason why she never heard back after submitting her FoodieLand auditions, though the camcorder seemed decent enough to me.

I hadn't asked for anything of the sort, not when it must've been outrageously expensive, but in that moment, I just knew fate and my birthday wish had collided. As I read up on the camera's features, thoughts of auditions were far from my mind—I was too busy dreaming of an oversized one million dollar check with my name printed on it.

3

Emmett refused to come on the boat ride. Getting to stay home alone must've been one of those perks of being thirteen.

It felt like breaking the birthday tradition to go on the ride without my brother, but at least the rest of us could fit in Papa's truck together without him. I squished up next to Gramps and watched him fiddle his thumbs together on the truck drive to the marina. East Cypress Drive was bumpy as we made our way out of town. The truck rattled and smelled like oil and Papa's cologne. I kept a tight grip on the new camera case as I held it on my lap.

Unlike last June when a lot of plants had fried to a brown crisp because of the drought, the weeds sprouted green and tall from the recent rain. They didn't compare to the trees though, especially not the great cypress with Spanish moss streaming from their soaring branches. The sun had lowered in the sky, giving them an even more grand appearance.

I took the camera out of the case to shoot a few practice pictures, but they came out blurry. I needed to tinker with the settings and learn all the special features later. I put the camera back in the case for now.

When we got close to the Polk St. Bridge across from downtown Jefferson, Papa turned down a road running parallel to Big Cypress Bayou and parked. I missed a step getting out of the truck, and Gramps helped steady me.

The marina was just a small wooden shack with a pair of pontoon boats tied up out back. There wasn't much inside the building except for a card table with three chairs that functioned as a desk, a game-head of a buck, spare boat parts, and several file cabinets. The Cypress Swamp Marina sign was missing off of the front door, and in its place, a homemade poster read, "Raleigh's Tours."

Mama must've noticed it at the same exact moment as me. "What in the name of—"

"The marina belongs to us now, which is why—"

Swamp Sam burst out of the office carrying the game head and a bag slung over his shoulder. He'd lost weight since the last time I saw him, but he hadn't bought a smaller size of clothes yet. His t-shirt and jeans practically melted off of him. Swamp Sam's face looked like he had acne or the chicken pox.

"Beware of Bigfoot! You should listen to me and shut the place down to keep the authorities off our backs, but do whatever helps you sleep at night," he said, tossing Papa a jingly set of keys.

Beware of Bigfoot and of the authorities? Had he forgotten to take his medication?

"What's this all about?" Mama asked as Swamp Sam headed for his brown truck that had to be older than the legend of Bigfoot.

"Swamp Sam has been a little … all around eccentric lately, and he decided to shut down the marina. I didn't want to lose my job, so I talked him into letting me buy the place at cost instead."

As they argued about Papa's rash decision, I found out why Gramps had been acting odd. Okay, not like Swamp Sam odd, but unlike himself. He'd loaned Papa the little bit of money he'd set away after retiring, and he'd agreed to help out with tours and administrative stuff.

"How could you both keep this from me?" Mama pulled her hair back into a tight ponytail and acted like she was about to scream. But she did something worse—she bawled.

Both Papa and Gramps tried consoling her with comments like "everything will be fine" and "it's alright, you'll see."

They sure didn't convince me. I wished Emmett would've been there so I didn't have to go through this alone. He would've made a joke or said something to lighten the mood.

Mama gathered herself together enough to speak. "What about my cooking dreams? What about the kids? We're barely making it as it is." Then she looked in my direction and pursed her lips like she shouldn't have said those things in front of me. But it wasn't anything I didn't already know.

"Things are going to change soon," Papa said, trying to sell us on how much money-making potential the marina had.

The only one who seemed to agree was Gramps. Mama went silent.

I wanted Papa to be right. We all NEEDED Papa to be right.

"Can we skip the boat ride and go home?" I asked once things calmed down a bit.

"Nonsense!" Gramps said. "Everything will be fine, and the tradition shouldn't stop now because of a few changes. What would Chuck Norris or your Gram do?"

"Stay, I guess," I said. Gramps knew what to say to get me to change my mind even if I wanted to be home. Papa had obviously gone to some trouble for my sake and had tied balloons to the roof posts on one of the pontoon boats. Pink, my favorite color from when I was five years old.

I expected Mama to put up some kind of fight, but she hadn't shifted out of silent mode. After we put on our safety vests, Mama took a seat on the bench near the railing.

Bugs floated near the edges of the water, and I swatted some away when we boarded the boat. Just as I was about to sit on the opposite side, Papa announced, "You ready to be my co-captain, Everdil?" Emmett had surely given him that idea.

"That doesn't seem safe," Mama said, breaking her silence.

"Emmett did just fine, and I know Everdil will do great too."

I sure hoped he was telling the truth. Mama held my camera for me as I took my place at the wheel. My hands grew damp as Papa revved the engine and flipped on the boat light. I paid close attention when he showed me how to work the throttle and steer the boat.

Papa sat near me and popped up to help correct the wheel when I steered to the right instead of the left. "Turn it that way. A little more. There you go. Imagine you're pushing a grocery cart at the store."

Truth be told, I once accidentally knocked over a pork-and-beans display with a grocery cart. The cans crashed down and rolled as far as the produce section.

It was hard to pay attention to Papa's advice when Mama and Gramps discussed finances and the future in the back of the boat. The wheel slipped out of control. *Focus*, I told myself and used Papa's tips to help me maneuver the pontoon boat to the center of the waterway.

As I sped up, the motion created a light breeze. The moon was visible in the sky even though the sun hadn't quite set. It would've made a great picture had the camera been handy.

The scenery seemed to calm everyone down somewhat, and Papa used this time to train Gramps using his official Captain Raleigh spiel.

"My fair guests," Papa said, "Caddo Lake was named for the Caddo Indians who settled this area. People have lived around here for hundreds of years. Tens of thousands even."

Gramps repeated him word for word, and added. "Chuck Norris was alive then. Death just hasn't had the courage to collect him yet."

Mama barged in, saying, "You're both distracting Everdil. She should slow down."

"Everdil is doing great." Papa continued, "After the Civil War, folks flocked here in pursuit of peace, but their good fortune was forever changed in 1873. This place used to be the only river port in Texas, but when a log jam was removed up north called the Great Red River Raft, the water levels here dropped immediately, making it impossible for steamboats to pass through. The population dropped off too, especially if Chuck Norris was involved," he added for Gramps' sake, "though it is still home to a few people and many creatures. Why, look yonder!"

I followed the direction of Papa's flashlight which revealed a triangular-shaped head skimming above the water, eyes practically glowing. A huge gator! That thing was so large it could take a person out. What a rare sight for Big Cypress Bayou!

The gator glided near us, checking to see if we were a threat. Good thing my gourmet dinner party didn't work out or else we'd reek of fried gator. When we floated by, the gator dunked under to swim away, causing the water to ripple in its leave.

"Straighten out. Even more," Papa said, and as I maneuvered the boat back to the center, he babbled on about how the bayou served a purpose in the Confederate War efforts.

Gramps repeated after Papa less and less. I tuned him out as I searched the coastline. That's when I saw someone climbing over the knobby cypress roots along the banks. The light was dim, but it was a tall man. I thought he might've been wearing a dark coat, but it was too difficult to see.

Papa is over six feet tall, and this person seemed a foot or so taller. The man glided through the edge of the swamp with as much ease as our pontoon boat cut through the water. Who would be walking this far out here and why? The wetlands were dangerous and difficult to climb through.

"Everdil, listen to your father, and watch where you're going!" Mama yelled.

Right as the man disappeared behind some cypress trees, a realization avalanched on me. This was no human being.

"BIGFOOT!"

4

Papa flew to the side of the boat like he was trying to get a good look at Bigfoot. I glanced over at Mama to see if the camera was within reach. The pontoon boat swerved.

"Everdil, careful!" Gramps fussed.

The boat stopped handling like a shopping cart and was now more like a hockey puck sliding on ice, but I refused to slow down. Not when Bigfoot lurked this close and a million dollars was at stake!

The shadowy twilight made it challenging to see along the banks, but the tall figure lurked less than the length of a football field away. I strained to get a better visual.

The manlike beast stepped out from behind a tree. His eyes flashed. And then they locked right on mine. His lips pulled back into a snarl, revealing fangs so sharp they could gnaw into me like

I was a bacon wrapped scallop.

"Over there!" I pointed again and jerked the wheel. "Pass me the camera, quick!" The boat veered in the wrong direction.

My shaky hands tried fixing the wheel out but sent the boat even more in the wrong direction. It now headed toward the banks and those menacing fangs.

Mama cussed, and Gramps one-upped her. Papa reached to take control of the wheel, but it was too late.

The four of us screamed as the boat slammed into a thick stretch of mud. A loud grinding noise flooded my ears as we hit the roots of a cypress tree. The crash tossed us forward, balloons bopping in the air. I admit to saying a few bad words myself, but luckily it went unnoticed.

Once I regained my balance, I threw the throttle into reverse and accelerated.

Papa moved me out of the way to turn the engine off. "Stop! You'll overheat the engine and churn mud into it."

"I'm sorry." I hunkered down on the red bench near Mama. She was okay and held onto the camera case so tight her fingers had turned as white as those awful fangs had been.

Leave it to Gramps to chuckle at a time like this. "Well, you won't find training like that in any manual. Nope, that's what you call on the job training, Chuck Norris style."

I didn't find his comment funny. Not then. Probably never. I could've seriously hurt the people who meant the most to me.

Papa spotlighted the banks. The glow from the flashlight revealed his concern. "We're stuck until the engine settles down."

"Maybe Bigfoot will rescue us like he supposedly rescued Tim's dad," Gramps said, chuckling all over again.

Mama checked his head over to make sure he hadn't hit it. "I'm fine, Macy," he said. "Just haven't had this much excitement in a while."

In the distance, a twig snapped. I shivered even though it had to be at least eighty degrees outside. After seeing those teeth, Bigfoot seemed more inclined to kill than help. Emmett was home alone, and he'd never know the real story of what happened to the rest of his family.

My brother was right. I ruined everything. Tears burned my eyes.

Mama checked me all over for injuries, too. "What in the world were you thinking, Everdil?"

"I guess I wasn't after I spotted Bigfoot."

Mama continued to give me a thorough inspection before hugging me. "I bet it was some poacher in the area. You remember that hiker who got shot?"

"No poacher is that tall and huge!" Here we were in the great wide open, but my lungs gasped for air like a fish plucked out of the water. If only I'd been able to grab the camera in time. I unzipped the camera case to check on it. Fortunately, Mama's tight grip had saved the camera from breaking or flying off the boat when we hit land.

"It's dark enough that you could've spotted a balloon out of the corner of your eye or imagined something after that television show and Gramps' tale. Not to mention your father's nonsense," Mama said.

"Doubtful," Gramps said which set Mama off. While she ranted about the mess we were in, I wondered if my brain had somehow tricked me into seeing things. Could those fangs have just been a figment of my imagination? Was I losing my mind like Swamp Sam?

No way.

Papa scouted the area with a flashlight while I surveyed the area in case Bigfoot tried to stealthily approach us. The engine still felt like it was on because I vibrated from nerves.

I about fell off the bench when a booming sound filled the air—like a boulder smacking against a dense tree trunk. "What was that?" I whispered. I snapped a picture, hoping whatever lurked out there would be afraid of the flash.

"Everdil, put the camera away before you scare me to death." Papa jumped off the boat and onto the muddy banks.

"What are you doing, Raleigh?" Mama asked. "There could be other gators around."

"I have to get the boat back into the water somehow." Papa

dug his feet into the mud and pushed the grounded boat. It barely budged. There was no way he'd be able to move the boat alone. Gramps joined him, and I had to do everything I could to help since I'd caused this trouble.

I kept my thoughts off of Bigfoot and gators as I jumped out of the boat. I wobbled when I landed on the soft ground.

Mama hesitated before following my lead. For someone who was trying to convince me there was no Bigfoot, she sure inspected the area. Then again, I'd just crashed the boat, and we were stuck here for who knows how long while my brother was home alone.

All of us positioned ourselves at the front of the boat and pushed. "I'm so sorry," I said over and over. I probably said sorry on my birthday more times than I had in all my twelve years put together.

After our fifth or sixth attempt, the pontoon boat gave a bit, scraping against the ground and the roots. We shoved it again right at the same moment another mysterious knock sounded. That freaky noise seemed to give us supernatural strength. We pushed the boat back into the water and crawled aboard.

"How can you explain those noises?" I asked Mama as we huddled together while Papa cranked the engine. She reached for my hand, and even though I'd turned twelve today, I clung to her.

"A large tree frog?" Mama guessed.

As I told her that tree frogs make noises like *quank!quank!*, not loud knocks, the engine churned and reeked of gasoline.

"I bet Bigfoot felt threatened and was trying to scare us off," Gramps said.

"No way," Mama said.

After another attempt, Papa finally got the engine to hum to life. "The boat might be scratched up, but it doesn't look like there's any major damage," he said, backing out of the mud trap while Gramps directed him. I'd been rightfully demoted as co-captain.

"I'm really, really, really sorry," I said as Papa guided us back to the marina.

"The blame belongs to your father more than it does to you, though I hope you've learned your lesson."

"Yes, ma'am."

My lungs clenched up again. The last thing I wanted was to make things worse between my parents. The silence on our ride home felt like an awful form of torture where I kept reliving my failure. I'm not just talking about almost destroying the boat and hurting my family—if I'd been able to capture a clear picture of the beast, this would've been a victory ride instead. We would've won the contest before those professional hunters in California stood a chance or anyone else who was looking, for that matter.

My birthday wish haunted me.

It was late by the time we dropped Gramps off at his cabin and then pulled into our driveway. I expected Emmett to peek out of his room and ask us what took us so long to get home, but he must've fallen asleep.

As Mama and Papa moved into the kitchen to talk things over, I banged on Emmett's door almost as loud as those knocks we'd heard outside. Not really, because that noise wasn't human. No matter how much Mama tried to dismiss those noises, there was only one real explanation.

Emmett still didn't answer. I had so much to say, and who knew when he'd talk to me again. I dug out some school supplies from my desk and scribbled how Papa now owned the marina along with Gramps and explained how I'd seen Bigfoot. I admitted I'd driven the boat and crashed it, even though it made me cringe to do so. Emmett would never let me live it down.

I slipped the two page letter under his door before getting ready for bed.

My room was as safe as could be, but the bright pink floral wallpaper closed in on me, like the most overgrown rose garden you could imagine. I stretched out in bed and took a few deep breaths in an attempt to relax. That was hard to do given tonight's events, plus Mama and Papa were arguing down the hall in their room.

I curled up with my stuffed pig collection and put the pillow over my head to block everything out. Neither helped. The bayou scene kept replaying in my mind. I sat up and scrolled through the pictures on the camera at least a dozen times.

I'd been so close. So, so close. I had a mission to seriously prove Bigfoot was real now. Not even the thought of those sharp fangs or the way that beast had stared me down could change my mind.

5

Claws gripped me by the shoulder and thrashed me about. "Help!" I cried, trying to run away from being mauled to death.

"Shh," Emmett said. "And wipe your mouth. You're drooling."

I sat upright in bed. I'd been asleep for a while—the clock on the nightstand read a quarter after ten in the morning. When I rubbed my face with the back of my hand, I almost called my brother Snagglemouth like some of the guys on his football team do. I thought better of saying it because my front tooth overlaps too, just not as much, and I *had* been drooling. Besides, Emmett and I had a lot to discuss. "Did you read my letter?"

Emmett rolled his eyes. "Why else would I be talking to you, Everdil Pickle Breath? Start explaining."

And so I did. Emmett grilled me with so many questions that

I repeated the entire story—telling him about the drive, the weird encounter with Swamp Sam, the news about the marina, seeing Bigfoot, and yes, crashing the boat. I choked and churned just like the engine when I came to that part.

Emmett smirked, and then his eyes narrowed. "How is it that you saw Bigfoot and no one else did?"

"I had an advantage at the front of the boat. Gramps believes me. I'm telling you the truth, Emmett. I'd swear on my own life, not just yours." If I had a Bible in my room, I would've placed my hand on it like people do on those courtroom TV shows. I held out my little finger to do a pinky promise instead.

Emmett said that was too girlie, and right as I spat in my palm to shake on it instead, he shook his head. "You're disgusting, Everdil."

When it came to my brother, I couldn't do anything right. "Fine, but I know what I saw. With Bigfoot this close, we have a decent chance of winning the contest."

Emmett stood there in the middle of my room, rubbing his chin like Papa has a tendency to do, only Emmett has a wimpy amount of chin fuzz instead of dark prickly stubble. "We should start by talking to Tim. He's as much a Bigfoot expert as his dad. You better shower first," he said, waving his hand in front of his nose. He grinned when I threw a stuffed pig at him.

As he turned around to leave, I said, "Hey, I'm sorry about what I said and smashing the cake in your face. At least it was the best frosting in the world."

Emmett nodded in acknowledgment, and his face softened like

he was about to apologize too. "I can't believe you're not grounded until high school. You really are a rotten sister, Everdil, but if we win the Bigfoot contest I promise I won't say that ever again."

As if I wasn't already motivated! I wasn't thrilled with the idea of involving Tim and his dad, but last night proved I couldn't do this alone.

After showering, I got dressed in a camouflage t-shirt and cutoff jean shorts, the same kind of stuff I wore most of the time. For some reason, thinking about seeing Tim made me start to sweat—and not because I'd taken an extra warm shower. No, it had to do with that hand incident.

I cringed all over again as I thought about what had recently happened. Emmett, Tim, and I had been hanging out after our last day of school. Tim kept walking closer and closer, his shoulder bumping into me once or twice. Right as Emmett skipped rocks across Caddo Lake, Tim held his hand out toward me. Without thinking, my fingers reached for his, and as soon as we touched, my skin zinged.

But to my horror, Tim had only been offering me a piece of gum. Emmett turned around at that moment. Tim dropped the gum on the ground, backing up from me like I'd come down with a swamp plague. I'd been avoiding him since.

I changed into my camouflage tank instead of the t-shirt. It's not like it was more fashionable or anything, but at least I didn't feel as toasty.

Mama and Papa weren't around, and I wondered where they

were, then I saw a note on the kitchen table. They both left to work the early shifts and wrote that if we needed anything to call them. I couldn't believe they left me alone after how much I messed up yesterday, but times were tough.

In case my apology wasn't enough, I cooked breakfast for Emmett. Turns out there's an art to breaking eggs. I accidentally smashed one into the bowl. Picking out the eggshell shards took a while, and I lost patience waiting for the pan to preheat. I cranked up the heat until the element below the stainless steel pan glowed red. When I poured the mixture in, the eggs sizzled as if they'd been dipped into a hot fryer. They didn't just scramble, they scorched.

"It smells like a stink bomb went off," Emmett said when he joined me in the kitchen.

"I made you breakfast. Unless you like eggs very well done, it's the thought that counts, right?" I said before I pitched my attempt.

Emmett shook his head in disbelief. "Leave it to you to mess up even the simplest of meals. Even Chuck Norris couldn't unscramble those eggs."

I tried to keep a serious face as I said, "Unlike her precious sous chef, Mama's cooking genes passed me over."

If you know how hard it is to clean burned eggs from the bottom of a stainless steel pan, you have my sympathies. By the time I washed and dried the pan, Emmett had put on one of Mama's many cupcake themed aprons and whipped us up crepes. Yes crepes, because that's my brother for you. He didn't seem to think any of *that* was too girlie.

Mama would've been especially proud of Emmett's breakfast. The crepes tasted flawless and so buttery that I almost started drooling again.

"Do you remember one of Gram's favorites?" Before Emmett had a chance to guess, I answered, "Chuck Norris can cut a knife using butter."

This made Emmett smile again, and in case he still had some hard feelings, I swiped a cream cheese rose from the doomed cake and added it to my plate.

"Not a bad idea," Emmett said, grabbing several frosting roses himself.

We both had a sugar buzz after gobbling up more frosting and downing the rest of the crepes. When Emmett called Tim, I had more dishes to wash and then responded to Mama and Papa's note.

I wrote out the last part of my letter larger than the rest so they'd focus more on that than how much I messed up. I drew an enormous smiley face for the same reason. Before we left, I made sure to bring the camera.

The walk to Tim's had me sweating even more. The humid air wrapped around my skin like a soggy bandage. It had to be at least ninety degrees. I glanced around after sensing someone was watching me but didn't see anything unusual, just an older couple out walking a fluffy white dog. I photographed the dog, only he ruined the shot by hiking his leg on a tall weed.

Mr. Nash and Tim live close to the lake near a section of older houses and cabins that tourists sometimes rent. Caddo Lake is peaceful and pretty, but Uncertain wouldn't be my idea of a vacation spot. If I had a chance to go anywhere, I would've picked an amusement park with roller coasters. Shawna had promised we'd visit Six Flags together after she moved to Dallas, but that never happened. She blew me off every time I hinted at visiting.

Emmett had nothing to say to me, so I thought of some food related trivia based on a show called Garbage Can Gourmet. Contestants are presented with a copper trashcan containing unlikely ingredients they must make into a gourmet meal. The contestants can use the studio's fully stocked kitchen to help, but the trashy ingredients must be the star of the dish. Anyway, Emmett liked Garbage Can Gourmet a lot, and I listed some items that might stump him. "Potato peels, that sugary part at the bottom of a cereal box, sweet tea, and an old box of raisins.

Quick, what would you make?"

"The Ingredient Game, huh," Emmett said. He stopped for a moment to stretch in the same way he warmed up before a football game. "Cinnamon raisin potato bread. With cream cheese frosting. Hit me again."

I couldn't shake the feeling of being tracked somehow, so it took me a moment to come up with the next batch of ingredients. "Okay—pre-cooked hamburger patties, Halloween gummy eyeballs, a packet of ketchup, and rusty lettuce."

"Easy! I'd cook taco soup."

Our Ingredient Game ended when we reached Tim's place. The door swung open right as we were about to ring the doorbell. I drew in my breath.

"What's up?" Tim said, looking right at me.

I turned away to stare at a spiderweb in the doorframe as if it was the most interesting thing ever. Tim's thick brown hair had grown out and needed a good brushing. He'd stretched out several inches taller than Emmett this last year which I found strange considering Mr. Nash is much shorter than Papa. Given our family histories, it seemed Emmett would've hit his growth spurt first.

"Nice necklace, Everdil," Tim said.

"Uh, thanks." I stepped forward to check out the spiderweb at such close range that I'm lucky the spider kept from jumping on my nose.

"That's our newest resident, a spiny backed orb weaver,"

Tim said, mentioning a few facts about the spider as he greeted Emmett with a complicated handshake.

I knew the hand motions, but kept my hands at my side to avoid any additional embarrassment, even as we walked inside the house. This threw my balance off, and I tripped over one of the many pairs of shoes scattered in the front entryway. I braced myself by hugging the wall to keep from face planting in a pair of tennis shoes. So much for not being embarrassed.

To make matters worse, Tim said, "Have a nice trip, Everdil. See you next fall!"

"Ha, ha. Let's get to business," I said after steadying myself.

Apparently, we'd missed Mr. Nash—he had to work today, too. The living room was as junky as the entryway, and there wasn't much room to talk and make plans. Thick science texts covered the coffee table, and the furniture functioned like a closet of sorts with stacks of folded laundry. I made sure not to knock over a tall pile of clean shirts next to me on the loveseat, especially when I used my hands to explain what had happened last night.

"I'm glad you're okay, but too bad you didn't get a picture," Tim said.

"No kidding." I scrolled through some of my practice pictures to continue avoiding his eye contact. I backed up to the picture I'd taken last night after the boat crash. I hadn't noticed it when I looked through the pictures before, but a minuscule spot of light stood out in the blackness. "Hey, look at this," I said, holding out the camera. Sure enough, I knocked over the stack of laundry piled next to me. Shirts tumbled off the loveseat and onto the floor.

"Don't worry about it," Tim said when I jumped to pick up the clothing. Several pair of briefs, both men's and boys', were curled up under the shirts.

No way was I going to touch those things! Before I moved, Tim lunged to cover up the laundry, our heads cracking together. Ouch.

He'd caught me so off guard that I stumbled. When Tim helped me get up, I was forced to look him in the eyes. Blood rushed out of my brain and into my cheeks.

"Sorry about that," he said.

"It's o—"

"Everdil would find a way of falling even if she'd been sitting on the couch," Emmett said. He must not have seen the underwear.

"Gee, thanks."

"So what were you going to show us?" Tim asked. His face was sunburn red.

Oh, yeah. I showed Tim and Emmett the picture, but neither one of them could see what I was talking about. It didn't help that Emmett smudged his fingerprints on the screen. He wiped the screen with his t-shirt only he smeared his finger grease worse.

"We should download the picture on the computer so we can zoom in," Tim suggested. He picked up the remaining piles of shirts scattered in the living room, and we headed into Mr. Nash's office.

This was the one and only organized room in the house.

Several pictures of Tim's mom hung on the wall before she graduated to Heaven when he was a baby. Carefully framed newspaper clippings of Bigfoot sightings also decorated the wall including one that had appeared in our local paper last year. The title read "Uncertain Sighting," where, supposedly, an elderly woman saw an ape walking upright at Caddo Lake State Park. I'd kind of thought the lady must've been senile or something, but not so much anymore.

Emmett grabbed a white object off of the top of the desk while Tim removed the memory card from the camera and inserted it into the computer's card reader. The object resembled the bottom of a foot. I squinted and counted the toes—four or maybe five.

"It's a cast Dad made of a print he recently found at the park. It had been raining and some plant roots got in the way," Tim said, explaining why it looked weird.

And speaking of weird, the picture finished downloading. So that minuscule light? When Tim zoomed in, it looked like a set of glowing eyes.

6

"That's got to be bogus," Emmett said, moving his big head in front of the computer screen to get a closer look.

I elbowed him out of the way. "You didn't see me tamper with anything. Like I'd even know how." Well, I could probably figure things out eventually, but that's not the point.

Tim moved in closer to me, and I wasn't sure if I should take a step back or stay put. The last thing I wanted was another lump on my forehead. Tim kept enough distance that I forced myself to stop worrying about it.

Tim clicked through several files saved on the computer. "Dad took a similar picture after he set up night vision trail cameras around the park. Here, look." Tim zoomed in on a trail camera photo that was amazingly similar to the one I'd taken—a pair of almond-shaped eyes shimmering against the pitch blackness.

The resemblance was enough to warp my skin into gooseflesh. "We should send these photos into the contest!"

"They're weird—really weird—but they don't prove anything," Emmett said.

I hated that he was right. Tim looked the contest rules up on the computer just to be sure. "The picture must be clear enough to prove Bigfoot's existence by a panel of experts who will thoroughly review all entries," he read aloud. Like on TV, a warning popped up on the computer. "Cryptic Cryptid Productions is not responsible for any related attacks or injuries."

While the picture wasn't enough to snag the million dollars, it was enough to get us more pumped to take a photo that would be worthy of recognition and money.

"We can be Team Bigfoot," I said, half-joking.

"Team Bigfoot. I like that. If we discover something, people will take my dad and me more seriously. Some of the scientific community thinks my dad is crazier than Swamp Sam," Tim said, and then he smiled. "Remember how we used to play Monster?"

I laughed thinking about it. Tim, Emmett, Shawna, and I played this lake game when we were little where we'd pat mud and green duckweed all over our swimsuits. Then we'd hang Spanish moss from our heads and would sneak up on Gram or Gramps. They'd pretend to scream, and we'd laugh like it was the funniest thing ever.

"Unlike Monster, Team Bigfoot will be the real deal," Emmett said, holding out his hand to shake on it.

Just when Tim went to shake my hand in return, I stalled. "We, uh, should have, uh, rules," I said.

"What kind of rules?" Tim asked, putting his hand into his pocket.

Good question. I hadn't thought the rule thing all the way through, so I took a moment to brainstorm. Finally, something came to me. "First," I said, imitating Papa's Captain-spiel talk to sound extra official, "we need to keep this a secret between the three of us. Other people will complicate matters, and then we'll have to split the money more ways. Second—" I tried to brainstorm another rule, but my mind blanked.

Tim helped me out. "We should prepare for anything." He must've taken the warning seriously, too.

"And third," Emmett said, "no one gets left behind." He looked right at me as he said, "Mama and Papa would never forgive me if I let something happen to their little baby."

I figured it was more like the other way around. We'd be fine, so I didn't have to worry about the second and third rules. I held out my hand to finally shake on it. Emmett squeezed my fingers so hard that one of my knuckles popped. Yeah, I could really tell he was going to look out for me.

I closed my eyes before shaking Tim's hand as if I was

expecting a shock instead of simply sealing the deal. His grip was much lighter than Emmett's but far more clammy.

The deadline was June fifteen, now only nine days away. Team Bigfoot had some plans to make.

We tinkered around on the Internet for information, and Tim showed us a few other suspicious looking pictures of dark creatures in the night that his dad had taken using trail cameras. He also showed us a famous video filmed by these guys named Patterson and Gimlin. The footage showed Bigfoot walking through the woods on a sunny day. The creature in the film didn't look all that threatening compared to what I'd witnessed. "Some people think it's a hoax, but others don't," Tim said.

If that video wasn't enough to prove Bigfoot's existence, we agreed that we needed something extraordinary. It had to be next to impossible, but not trying seemed worse than trying and failing.

I volunteered to make a list of items we needed.

- camera
- first aid kit
- water bottles
- flashlights
- pocket knife
- compass
- backpacks
- hiking boots
- camouflage clothes

"You've got that last item covered, Everdil," Emmett said. He and Tim laughed at my wardrobe choices.

"Can you add some chips to that list?" Tim asked. "And beef jerky? Like the biggest container possible. Oh, and some granola bars, a lot of them. And maybe a package of cherry chews."

I must've been looking at him funny because he said, "What? I can't stop eating these days."

"We might as well get a box of cookies, too. Apparently an economy sized box of cookies," Emmett added.

"You're not going to make us some cookies from scratch?" I asked.

Emmett play-slugged my arm. Some of Emmett's football teammates had teased him after he'd brought homemade cookies to practice. One of the guys said Emmett was destined to be the next great short order cook at Uncertain Café, and ever since then, Emmett had gotten sensitive about his culinary aptitude. Tim got teased about wanting to be a scientist like his dad, but he knew how to roll with it, unlike my brother.

"If I do cook something, I won't bring anything for you, brat," Emmett said.

"I was just kidding," I said and hoped that he'd quickly forget this part of the conversation. Whatever snack Emmett made would be a thousand times better than anything I could scare up in the pantry.

Tim must've gotten tired of our arguing because he suggested, "I say we gather our things together and bike over to the park."

"Sounds good," I answered, sounding like a suck up. Or at least Emmett looked at me like I was one. Regardless, starting at Caddo Lake State Park made a lot of sense given the reported sightings, plus we'd be able to ask Tim's dad some questions.

"Why don't you meet us over at our house, then?" Emmett said to Tim. When we gathered our things to leave, he stopped in his tracks. "You know, there's something that doesn't make sense to me."

"What?" Tim and I asked at the same moment. Had this happened before the hand incident, I would've tapped his arm and said, "Jinx."

"Why would Swamp Sam just up and sell the marina like he did? Maybe there's more to his craziness. You think he knows something about Bigfoot that we don't?"

He made a darn good point. Maybe Swamp Sam's latest fear of the authorities was just a cover story for his true intentions. Before he started getting obsessed with Bigfoot, Swamp Sam's whole life revolved around the marina and fishing. He was old, but not ancient, and he probably had a good reason to sell the marina to Papa. Like maybe a million-dollar-Bigfoot-contest-idea.

Team Bigfoot made the decision to pay Swamp Sam a visit first before going to the park.

"See you at our house in a little bit," I told Tim as we left.

"Yeah," he said, looking down. Did he ever replay the hand incident in his mind like I did? Was he afraid of giving me the wrong impression? *Quit over-thinking things and focus on the*

Bigfoot mission instead, I told myself.

The walk from Tim's house seemed much quicker than on the way there and the heat didn't seem to bother me as much either. I mentally went through our checklist—gather some food, water, and other items, and then pull our bikes out of our packed garage.

But as we got near our house, our mission had been majorly compromised.

7

A girl sat on our stoop with a large bag propped up near the door. Her face was familiar, yet not, considering the many layers of makeup coating her eyes and lips, plus she had burgundy highlights streaked throughout her long strands of dark hair.

"Hey, guys!" the girl called out. While she looked different than I remembered, there was no doubt the voice belonged to my former best friend.

"Shawna? What are you doing here?" I couldn't believe she was in town, at my house, sitting on our front stoop! Emmett held his mouth open so wide a horsefly could've easily zoomed in.

"Didn't your mom say anything?" Shawna stood up and towered over me. Shawna was a year older than me, and she very much looked like a teenager now. She'd grown slightly taller, yes, but unlike Tim's growth spurt, her height difference could be explained by her high wedge-heeled sandals. While her shoes had gotten taller, her skirt seemed to have shrunk, and her tight tank top showed off part of her tanned belly. Did she have curves like that before she left, or was she just showing them off more now?

Even though twelve wasn't that far from thirteen, I was nothing more than a little girl standing before her.

"I was supposed to come to your party last night, but Dad got delayed at work, like always."

"But you never replied to the invite ..."

"I did, but your mom had this idea about wanting to surprise you."

Emmett cleared his throat. "It's a nice surprise. You're being rude, Everdil."

"Sorry, things have been kind of ... crazy." I couldn't bring myself to fill Shawna in on the recent happenings.

I hugged her, and it felt like hugging someone you've met only a few times before, not someone who used to be your best friend. As Emmett hugged Shawna, her shirt rose up slightly. I expected to see her bellybutton pierced or something, but it sunk in like normal and was free of bedazzled jewelry.

Emmett kept staring at her until I knocked him in his arm.

"I can't believe you're here," I said. When was the last time we'd talked? Months, I supposed.

"You probably heard, but my grandma's not doing well. I'm back in town for part of the summer to help out, and your mom suggested I could stay here for a little while until Grandma gets settled at home."

Word had spread around town that her grandma had fallen, but I didn't think it was serious. Why hadn't my mom shared any of this with me?

"Here, let me help you." Emmett bent down to pick up Shawna's overstuffed bag and carried it inside the house.

"Whoa, Everdil," Shawna said when she stepped into my room. "Your room's exactly the same."

"So?" She hadn't been gone all that long, and it's not like my family had the kind of money that hers did to redecorate every five minutes.

"Don't get defensive. I just thought you might've added some posters or personality or whatever by now," she said, moving her stuff near my dresser.

As I struggled to think of something to say, the doorbell rang. Tim had arrived, just as we'd planned.

For some reason, I wanted to turn Tim away before he caught a glimpse of this brand new Shawna. She was closer to his age, and I still couldn't get over how teenager she looked. The front door smacked behind me as I rushed outside. Tim was setting his bike near the garage door, a huge backpack slung over his shoulder. "You guys ready?" he asked.

"About Team Big ... the adventure, we've had a change of plans and maybe—" I stopped cold when Shawna stepped out the door with Emmett.

Shawna rushed up to him, wrapping her arms around his neck. "You've gotten so tall, Timmy!"

She called him Timmy now. Seriously?

Emmett pivoted on his toes—was he trying to make himself look taller for her?

Tim stood with his arms by his sides like he didn't know what to do. "Uh, hi, Shawna. Are you home for good?" Was that hope I heard in his voice?

"My grandmother had a stroke and got out of the hospital two days ago. I'm staying with my mom for several weeks to help Grandma out as she learns how to walk and do stuff for herself again."

My emotions whirled around like they were on the spin cycle, and my heart hurt to hear about what had happened to her grandmother. With Gram, it had all been so sudden. Gram was alive and laughing one day, and then she doubled over and was gone the next. I'll always remember how Emmett stood up at her funeral and said, "I wish my grandmother could've been like Chuck Norris. His heart would never be dumb enough to attack him." Instead of laughing, he broke down. We all did. Mama comforted us by saying how Gram didn't suffer, and here Shawna's grandmother must've been suffering a lot. "Sorry," I whispered.

Shawna's charcoal-lined eyes smudged from her tears.

Emmett moved in to give her a hug. She returned his embrace but without the same warmth as she'd hugged Tim (now also known as Timmy). After a long pause, Emmett asked, "Should we get going?"

"What was that adventure you were talking about a moment ago, Everdil?" Shawna asked.

Just as I hadn't wanted Tim to see Shawna, I hesitated to include her in our Bigfoot plans. We'd made rules, after all. "Let's go swimming! Did you pack a swimsuit?"

"Of course. There's not much else to do in this lame town," Shawna said.

Tim nodded his head in response, and for some reason, it bothered me to think he agreed with her about the lameness of our town. I mean, if I'm being one-hundred percent truthful I'll admit I sort of agree, but still, Tim's two best friends live here. No matter what, it's *home.*

"I better go change then," Emmett said.

I'd been looking forward to catching up with Shawna, but we now had one less day to win the contest.

8

Turns out, Shawna had packed three swimsuits—bikinis, actually. All I owned was my ratty polka dotted one-piece, the backside pilled from sitting on our dock countless times.

Shawna changed in the bathroom while I stayed in my room, squeezing into my swimsuit and covering up with a worn t-shirt and an even more worn pair of jean shorts. The paper-thin fabric felt comfortable, but the shorts had frayed so much that long strings hung down and tickled my thighs when I walked. I almost forgot about the necklace so I turned around to take it off, setting it on the dresser for safekeeping.

It took about twenty minutes for Shawna to primp and change into her swimsuit-catalogue-type of bikini. When she made her debut out of the bathroom, I gawked at her. Shawna's hair was pulled back in a super-bouncy-burgundy-streaked-ponytail, and she'd freshened up her eyeliner. My parents would've thrown a fit if I looked so mature.

"This will be like old times," Shawna said, stopping in front of the hallway mirror to adjust her hair as we walked to meet up with the boys. From the flat tone of her voice, I wasn't sure if she thought that was a good or bad thing.

Tim and Emmett were waiting for us in the living room, tossing a foam football back and forth. Emmett had changed into his fluorescent orange trunks and yellow shirt still stained from the frosting. Tim hadn't borrowed anything from my brother, probably because they were two different sizes now. I guess he planned on swimming in his regular clothes.

Both of the boys stopped cold when they saw Shawna. When Tim launched the ball, it thudded against Emmett's chest.

I couldn't wait to get outside. "Race you all to the dock!" The back door smacked the wood frame behind me.

Our backyard wasn't fenced in, and neither was our neighbor's yard a couple of lots away. You could see Caddo Lake less than a mile from the porch. Cypress trees framed the lake and looked so strong, so sturdy, that it seemed like nothing could ever destroy them, not even time. I headed down the dirt footpath that led down a hill to the lake.

Tim started to say something about Bigfoot to me when Shawna called out, "Hey, wait up!" He ditched me without hesitation to help her, but Emmett rescued her first. Apparently, she'd stumbled over a rock in her tall sandals and had to pick up the purse she'd dropped. She never used to carry a purse. Had she forgotten what it was like to live here?

I turned around and walked the remaining distance to the dock alone. The wooden boards creaked when I stepped on them. The water was murky, and in some places, it appeared slimy green from the duckweed on top and because of the lily-pad-looking spatterdock. None of those things stopped me from canon-balling into the lake, shorts and shirt and all. The coolness of the water was a welcome distraction.

As soon as I popped up, little bits of duckweed stuck to my skin and my t-shirt suctioned to me as well. I worried it revealed too much, or in my case, too little. Why hadn't I thought about this before jumping in?

I dunked back under and swam to where the lake was shallow enough to stand yet deep enough to cover me. My feet sank into the mushy layers of mud. As I waited for the others to join me, the water rippled, and a whiny groan sounded. The memory of the fangs flashed in my mind.

"Are you messing with me, Emmett?" I said when he reached the dock.

"What are you talking about?"

And that's when something wrapped itself around my ankle. I stepped back. Whatever it was tightened, reminding me of the claw from my nightmare.

I screamed so loud a heron in a nearby tree flapped its wings.

My leg thrashed about.

"You okay?" Tim asked.

"Something's got me!" I kicked hard and the grip around my ankle loosened. This was no claw—I'd kicked up a huge plant. And the noise was nothing more than a passing jon boat. The fisherman gave me a funny look as he passed by.

"Everdil's got a case of the Swamp Sams. 'Something's got me,'" Emmett mocked.

Tim and Shawna laughed at me, and on the count of three, the boys jumped in, arms and legs flailing. The lake exploded in a plume of water. Shawna shrieked, and I nearly choked on a wave.

"Who had the biggest splash?" Emmett asked as soon as he surfaced.

"I think you did, but with all that water it's hard to te—"

"You guys soaked me!" Shawna inspected her purse to make sure her phone was okay and then pressed water from her ponytail. In summers past, she always joined us in the water. She could hold her breath underwater the longest out of the four of us—sixty-four seconds—and she even won our end of summer freckle award for having the most spots.

"Sorry," Tim said.

Emmett dunked under the water, and when he popped up, he wore a duckweed crown. He swiped his hand over his head and pulled a small clump off. "I'd forgotten the game of Monster until you mentioned it, Tim."

Shawna's laughter encouraged Tim. He dug up a clump of

fishy smelling mud, and then he smeared it up and down his arms, taking shelter by the canoes. Shawna had pulled her cell phone out of her purse when Tim acted like he was about to bomb her with a mud-ball.

Shawna covered up her cell phone. "Don't even think about it, Timmy! This phone is barely working as it is with the horrible cell coverage."

So I wouldn't go unnoticed, I plucked some spatterdock and swam over to Tim, placing the green discs on his back like he had some weird swamp disease.

Tim held his arms up as if he was a zombie-monster. "You're going down, Everdil!"

And with that, he dunked me under and swam off. As soon as I regained my breath, I zipped through the lake to get him back. When I caught Tim, I placed my arms on top of his bony shoulders and leaned in, trying to knock him over.

But he didn't budge. How was I supposed to respond next?

I backed up and splashed him. So much water slammed his face that he sputtered.

"Oops!"

Well, that ended things. While Tim washed the mud and the duckweed off the best he could in the lake, Shawna placed her phone back into her purse. I crawled onto the dock with the hopes that no one would notice how my wet clothes revealed my straight up and down frame.

As soon as I made it onto the warm wood, I peeled my shirt away from my skin and squeezed water from it.

Shawna scooted out of the way when Tim climbed onto the dock. Emmett spattered us with droplets of lake water. Shawna groaned in disgust. It didn't help my brother stunk like a toad.

Something growled, low and rumbly. "Did you hear that?" I asked, glancing near the cypress trees.

"Hear what?" Emmett asked.

"Shh," Tim said, "that could've been a vocalization."

There was another growl and then a great roar. *RRaawwrrrr!*

Shawna gasped and grabbed my arm. I about fell off the dock.

"It's just me," Gramps said, walking out of the trees, laughing so hard he snorted. "I got y'all good!" He did a double take when he saw Shawna. "So good to see that the Four Stooges have been reunited."

Gramps kicked off his shoes and joined us, swirling his feet in the water like he was one of us kids. "Your mama wanted me to check on you guys after the whole Bigfoot boat debacle."

"Bigfoot boat debacle?" Shawna asked.

"Didn't Everdil tell you she got a good look at the Caddo Critter?"

"He's just kidding," I said, regretting the words as soon as they came out of my mouth.

9

"How can you say Bigfoot is a joke, Everdil?" Tim asked, his eyes narrowed. "You of all people with your report and big talk."

Emmett jumped in. "You weren't lying to us, were you?"

"Of course not!" A speck of duckweed described how big I felt at that moment. "I ... I lied to avoid involving Shawna." I reached for my necklace. I panicked for a moment when the pearl wasn't there, but then I remembered I'd left it on my dresser.

"Why wouldn't you want me to get involved?" Shawna asked.

I shrugged. This was more than I could explain.

"Because I don't believe in Bigfoot?" Shawna continued when I stayed silent.

"I wasn't sure what I thought about Bigfoot until I got a firsthand look," I said. Sharing my experience wasn't violating any of Team

Bigfoot's rules, so I told her about everything that had happened.

Gramps filled her in on my boat driving skills. Or lack thereof.

"You might've been seeing things," Shawna said, sounding exactly like Mama.

"My eyes are fine, I promise."

"Yeah, they are," Tim said.

What in the world was that supposed to mean?

"Do you even believe in the *possibility* of Bigfoot? Thousands of credible people like Mr. Nash and Gramps do," Emmett said.

Gramps set an arm around Emmett's shoulder as if to show him some solidarity.

Tim has this nerdy tendency to go into encyclopedia mode, and he fully unleashed it now. "Did you know that researchers discovered a primate species named Omomyids amidst 42-million-year-old fossils south of us in Laredo?" he asked.

Tim took Shawna's shrug as an invitation to drop another fact. "Bigfoot might be related to the giant Asian ape called *Gigantopithecus blacki* that coexisted with humans over a hundred thousand years ago."

"So Bigfoot is basically an oversized panda," Shawna said, raising an eyebrow.

"A panda isn't an ape. Think really big gorilla capable of stomping on people's huts," Tim said.

"Like Godzilla," Emmett said.

Gramps chuckled. "Panda-Godzilla-Bigfoot. I can only imagine."

"We're losing focus," I said.

"Fine," Shawna said, "but why hasn't someone found evidence of a Bigfoot family living in the woods or Bigfoot bones or fossils?"

"Some scientists think they have, including my dad. I'll show you," Tim said, and then explained how hard the evidence can be to verify, especially with not much to compare it to.

"You're a chip off the ol' block," Gramps said, referring to Mr. Nash. "I have to get to the marina, but I'll be around if you need me. I'll report y'all are just fine to your mama. Before I go, I got a good one that Gram would've loved."

"What's that, Gramps?" I asked.

Gramps chuckled again before he could even get the joke out. "Chuck Norris keeps a Bigfoot rug in his room. Bigfoot isn't dead, he's just too afraid to move."

We all laughed.

"You're right," I said. "Gram would've loved it."

As soon as Gramps was out of earshot, Emmett told Shawna, "We plan on discovering some real evidence." Before I could stop him, he spilled the news about the contest.

"A million dollars for a photo? You've got to be kidding me."

Shawna had to know we weren't kidding by now, even if I'd tried to say so earlier.

"Look, you're free to think whatever, and you don't have to join us if you don't want to. Besides, it might be too dangerous," I said.

I'd given her an easy out, and when she stood up, I thought she might've stomped off to my room, but she surprised me by saying, "I could help."

"How?" I asked, my filter still down.

"It doesn't really matter. If Shawna wants in, she's in," Emmett said, standing up to shake her hand before checking in with Tim or me. "We'll split the money between all of us."

"She doesn't need the money like we do," I argued, but then Shawna interrupted me.

"Look, I can have my dad send some cash to help us out in the search," she said.

"But why would you?"

"I could use some distraction," she said, like that explained everything perfectly.

Money would help us buy some equipment so we wouldn't have to borrow everything from Papa. I didn't get a chance to think the decision through because Tim held out his hand and shook her onto our team. I'd been outvoted without the chance to cast my own ballot. "Fine, but Team Bigfoot has rules, and we're not going to break any more of them."

I confess I squeezed Shawna's hand a little harder than necessary, but to her credit, she didn't whine or back down.

All it took was one successfully sent text message, and Shawna's dad added money to her account. One text message and money just appeared from one place to another! Of course, she'd have to pick it up at the grocery store ATM, but still. Papa had slaved away at the marina for years and did all sorts of odd jobs and never had anything to show for it. Mama worked endless hours at the café and spent all of her remaining effort and funds on trying to make it big in the food industry, but nothing had happened yet. Having extra money seemed like it would never be a possibility for my parents. Not unless something MAJOR changed.

"I should look into becoming a lawyer someday," I said to myself, still marveling at how loaded her dad had to be to send money like that.

"Sure you might be rolling in it, but you'd never have any time to spend with your future kids," Shawna said. Before Shawna moved to Dallas, she'd only spent a few weeks here and there with her dad. It didn't seem like her plan to get to know him better was working out all that well.

Shawna put up her phone after sending her dad a message that simply said, "Thx."

As if she was the one in charge of our team, she said, "Let's plan how and when we're going to go get the money." And here she didn't believe in Bigfoot!

Mama and Papa had recently pawned their bikes to pay off a bill, so that complicated our plans for now. Shawna wouldn't get far in those ridiculous sandals of hers.

"Let's split up," Tim suggested. "Two of us can look more into Swamp Sam, and the other two can pick up money and maybe some supplies."

"I'll go with you, Shawna," Emmett said. His face broke out in blotches almost like he was having an allergic reaction. His breathing seemed fine enough, so I chalked it up to nerves.

Tim tinkered with a few small appliances before offering that he could go with her as well. What was this, some sort of competition within a competition to hang out with Shawna? They'd brought her on our team, and this was going to be a miserable hunt for Bigfoot if I didn't take charge.

"The boys will go snoop, and the girls will walk to the store," I said. "Shawna and I haven't spent time together in ages."

Before we parted, Shawna borrowed a pair of my sneakers. "These look … comfy," she said. Shawna frowned as she put them on.

Comfy was her nice way of saying my shoes were ratty, which was the truth. They were better than her breaking an ankle in those wedged sandals though.

Tim and Emmett had the more important task of stalking Swamp Sam, but our mission was important, too. "Hurry up!"

10

What seemed like it would be a quick stop at the grocery shop quickly turned into a disaster.

Shawna made some small talk about her new fancy pants middle school that had electronic this and that and everyone got assigned their own laptop. It had an enormous stadium that put our town's to shame. When school started in the fall, I'd attend the grade seven through grade twelve campus with the boys. I'd looked forward to it, but now our school felt like a joke in comparison.

I filled her in on what some of the kids at school were up to now, and then I asked her if she remembered when a skunk wandered into the elementary school gym and how everyone freaked out.

"You're younger than me, so it must've left a bigger impression."

"I'm not that much younger than you." I kicked a rock. "Do you remember how I gave you that stuffed fish that you named Minnoe the Minnow because of your last name?"

"Barely. We were such babies then."

After a stretch of uncomfortable silence, I said, "Emmett and I recently came up with what we call the Ingredients Game. If you were on that show Garbage Can Gourmet and someone gave you shrimp, candy corn, cheese curds, and a butternut squash, what sort of dinner would you make?"

Shawna wrinkled her nose in disgust. "Uh, a trash pile patty."

Her answer made me laugh. Shawna laughed too and relaxed her shoulders as we continued walking. I took several snapshots of the way the clouds reflected off of the lake. They came out quite artistic if I do say so myself.

We followed Blair Landing Road and soon passed Gramps' cabin, right near the water with a short wooden pier where he liked to sit.

Shawna must've noticed me staring at the cabin because she asked, "Your grandpa works at the marina now?"

I explained how Papa bought the place from Swamp Sam and hired Gramps.

"That's a good thing, right?"

I thought about how Mama reacted to the news. "Maybe. You probably remember how Bigfoot crazy Swamp Sam is—we have a suspicion he sold the marina thinking he might win the competition. That's why Emmett and Tim are going to find out more information so we can beat him to it."

"Makes more sense now," Shawna said, a touch out of breath since we were walking at a quick pace. "By the way, thanks for letting me join the team."

"It's not like I had much of a choice."

Maybe she was just getting sweaty from the walk, but Shawna looked on the verge of tears.

"Sorry, I didn't mean for that to sound rude."

Shawna stopped walking. "Look, Everdil. I'm sorry if I've hurt your feelings. When I moved to Dallas, I kind of wanted to reinvent myself, you know?"

"I wouldn't know anything about that." It hurt to know she'd purposely wanted to forget about me so she could have a better life. "Let's get this over with fast so we can meet up with the boys." I walked on, and she raced to catch up to me.

The grocery store in Uncertain is small compared to the ones you'll find in big cities, but it has just about anything you might need, including an ATM. "You think this will work?" I asked before we walked inside. Could a thirteen year old really just slide a card into a machine and get money out?

"How country are you? Of course this will work," Shawna said, standing taller and seeming more confident than she had moments before. "Dad got me the account and the card because he wanted to keep the extra cash a secret from Mom. I use it all of the time."

Shawna's parents divorced when she was young, and that's when Shawna's mom moved home to Uncertain to be closer to family. Shawna's parents had more money than either one of them probably knew what to do with. It surprised me that they'd fight over something like how much Shawna could spend, but adults can fight about anything, rich or poor. Take Mama and Papa for example.

As we neared the front of the store by the machine, Shawna smacked her lips together and adjusted her hair. "Does my makeup look okay?"

"If you're into that sort of stuff."

She rolled her eyes at me. "Hey Everdil, stop looking so nervous. People might think you're going to shoplift or something."

At the mention of "shoplift," I glanced around to see if anyone had overheard her. The last thing I wanted was for someone in town to get the wrong impression of me. Thankfully, no one paid me any attention. I didn't want to complicate the transaction, so I told Shawna I'd meet her in a few minutes.

I planned on waiting for her at the front of the store, but I spied a man who kind of looked like George Washington, only with dark hair instead of a white wig. I followed him to the meat case, shoving my hands in my pocket to avoid looking so ... thieving or whatever. I'd never seen him in Uncertain before, and trust me, I would've remembered. His khaki outfit had pockets galore and looked more appropriate for an African safari than out here in quiet, nowhere East Texas.

I crept near the case of cheese to get a better look at the man. He gave off this weird vibe.

"I'm here," the man said, tossing a pack of thick sliced bacon into his basket. A bony stub was all that was left of his middle finger.

"Huh?" I answered and then felt dumb because the man wasn't talking to me but rather into some headset piece that connected to his phone. To play my reaction off, I picked up a block of cheese with eyeball-sized blue chunks in it. I'd have to remember this for the Ingredient Game. The Founding Father lookalike glanced in my direction but kept on talking. He shook his head in annoyance.

"Some local mentioned seeing a large black creature slightly north of here earlier, but I think its baloney." Funny enough, the guy had moved on to the lunch meat section and stood close to several selections of bologna. Yet another item for the Ingredient Game.

I followed the man as he moved along, stopping to inspect some bags of shredded cheese with enough interest that I hopefully didn't look like a stalker.

The lookalike snickered at something. "You have no idea! This town is backwards, and the people are no exception." The man looked over at me again. My nostrils flared in response.

Swamp Sam was a potential danger, but he didn't seem as threatening as this man. To keep from drawing more attention to myself, I grabbed the only thing I could afford with the change in my pocket—an individually wrapped piece of string cheese. I sped off to the cash register, my mind racing just as fast.

Shawna and I would have to forget buying any supplies for

now. We had all we needed to win the contest—inside information and my camera. She and I had to head north of here before the presidential lookalike had a chance. We'd consult with Tim and Emmett later.

Shawna stood at the front of the store waiting for me as planned, though she raised her hands up questioningly as I stood in line to pay for the string cheese. When it was my turn, the man walked around the corner. We had to hurry.

I tossed my pocket change at the clerk, though most of it clanked on the ground.

The clerk sighed, and I tried picking up the quarters, but my fingers fumbled. Shawna came to my rescue, handing the clerk a dollar bill to pay for the cheese while I collected the remaining coins.

"You couldn't wait for a snack?" Shawna asked once we paid up.

I pocketed the string cheese for now and rushed her outside. "I'll tell you the story in the minute. I take it you got the money?"

"No problem at all." Shawna grinned as she reached into her pocket and flashed a stack of twenties. She kept it secret how much she'd taken from the account, but the stack was so thick it reminded me of a scene from a mob movie, just without any stealing or murder.

Shawna followed me north to Mound Pond as I shared what I'd overheard. I kept my camera out, almost like a weapon in case we stumbled onto something important ... or freaky.

"I saw that guy. He looks familiar, and I got an off feeling about him," she said.

SQUAWK! Shawna and I dropped to the ground, but the sound was only a crow. It swooped across the clearing to a tall pine.

"Gross!" Shawna said after we'd continued to walk quite aways. She'd stepped in something disgusting as she hiked through a stretch of mud.

Nasty—those were my shoes she was wearing, and they were now covered in rotted smelling goo. I pinched my nose as Shawna walked over to a rock and tried cleaning off my sneaker.

Off in the distance, I swear I saw something scuttle.

"Don't move," I whispered to her.

Shawna turned around. Something scurried again, only a stone's throw away.

A creature was crouched low to the ground.

It fit what I'd overheard that man in the grocery store describe.

Large.

Hairy.

Black-brown.

I aimed my camera at it. *Click.*

11

A large boar, bigger than Shawna and me put together, stepped out from the brush. Its tusks were a couple of inches long. The boar sniffed the air, stared at us, and charged.

"Stay calm," I told Shawna the instant we bolted for the trees. I slid the camera into my remaining free pocket. We needed to climb up a nearby oak if we were going to live through this.

Shawna's tree climbing skills weren't what they used to be— she could barely pull herself up the trunk, and then she stalled. "I broke a nail!"

"Who cares? Hurry up!" I hollered. She'd be a goner if she didn't. Or I might be since I was the one still stuck on the ground. These thoughts were enough for me to give her bottom a strong shove.

"Watch it, Everdil!" Finally, she was able to lift herself up the branch.

Something crackled, but it wasn't because Shawna was having issues climbing. The boar had gained on me.

Now that Shawna was higher up, I gripped the trunk and grabbed for a branch. It split off and sliced my upper arm. My brain triggered the pain, but I couldn't dwell on it, not when Shawna cried out, "Everdil!"

I made the mistake of looking back. The boar was only about twenty feet away, and here I was pressed against the tree like a human target. I jumped to the ground.

"Use the cheese," Shawna called out.

Good thinking. I pulled the string cheese out of my pocket and tried opening it. But the cheese had softened from my body heat, making the wrapper impossible to open. I tossed the entire package to the ground.

The boar sniffed it but must've been craving meat, not cheese. He barreled after me.

I tore off running to find a new tree for protection.

The cypress trees ahead would've worked, but they were too deep in swamp murk for me to get there in time. I stopped running when I found a rock on the ground.

Shawna yelled something, but I couldn't make out her words. The boar lunged in my direction, its jaws snapping. I was going to be porker chow if I didn't stand my ground.

"Get out of here!" I screamed as I kicked at the beast, shooting up a dirt cloud. Chuck Norris could've done way better. The boar grunted.

Visualizing how David took Goliath out with nothing but a slingshot, I chucked the rock at the bristly beast, thwacking its snout.

Another grunt.

Another charge.

Despite wanting to turn around and run for my life, I said a quick prayer. The only other option was to throw my new camera at it, but then I found a small stick near my foot. I grabbed it. With everything I had, I launched it at the boar. "I said get out of here!"

God did me a favor just like he had done for David. My attacker took off back into the brush.

I gulped for air when the beast was finally out of sight. Blood trickled from the cut on my arm. It wasn't too deep although the skin around it had started to puff up and turn purplish-red.

Shawna raced up to me. "You were amazing."

Minus her lack of climbing skills, she did okay too, but my voice quivered too much to tell her. We were lucky to walk away with only a cut and some scrapes.

That local who gave the George Washington lookalike that tip had been right—there was an enormous creature north of town, but Shawna and I could certify it wasn't Bigfoot.

While the man had unknowingly sent us on a wild hog chase, we were confident he wasn't going to find anything in this vicinity we hadn't. Well, except for a piece of string cheese on the ground. I wondered what he'd make of that.

As we trekked back to my house, alive and a wad of twenty dollar bills richer, my mind went back to Shawna's comments following the boar attack. I guess I was sort of awesome.

The sun had lowered in the sky by the time we made it back. Mama was the only one home. Emmett and Tim must've found a promising lead.

"It's so good to see you, Shawna!" Mama said, staring at her for almost a full minute before she embraced her. "I'm so sorry the surprise didn't go as planned and that I wasn't here to greet you earlier. I've been … distracted."

"Good to see you, too, Mrs. Jackson," Shawna said. "You look great."

That was nice of her to say because Mama was a mess. Dark circles outlined her eyes, and the odor of a long day of frying stuff, flipping burgers, and grilling onions hung to her jeans and t-shirt. "Where's Emmett?" she asked.

When I shrugged, Mama eyed the cut on my arm. "And what

happened to you?"

I pictured the boar's slashing jaws. There was no way I was going to tell her about the attack. I thought of how to respond without lying, but Shawna had that covered.

"Nothing like an old fashioned tree climbing contest," she said. "And if you compare cuts, you can tell that I won."

"That's not ..." I started to say to defend my honor, but Mama's laughter stopped me as did Shawna's glare.

"You girls may be growing up much too fast, but some things stay the same." Her gaze lingered on Shawna again. "Let's get you both cleaned up."

Mama grabbed the first aid kit. The alcohol wipes stung my arm, but I toughed it out just like Shawna did as she cleaned her scrapes. A large bandage completed my care. This is shameful, but I took pride that I needed one when Shawna didn't.

"You girls need to be more careful," Mama said.

No kidding.

Mama asked Shawna all kinds of questions as we moved into the kitchen to grab a bite to eat, mostly about how her family members were doing.

"We're okay," Shawna said, almost in a whisper. It was obviously something she didn't want to talk about, and Mama had the sense not to push the subject.

As tired as Mama had to be, she lit up as she grabbed some produce from the fridge like she was on Garbage Can Gourmet—a somewhat wilted cucumber, a tomato with a bruise on it, a tub of cream cheese, and a loaf of sourdough bread. She was born to be a chef. "I've been praying your grandmother makes a quick and complete turnaround," Mama said while slicing cucumbers so thin they were nearly transparent. "You can stay here as long as you need to. Everdil has missed you bunches. We all have."

I waited for Shawna to say she missed us too, but Shawna looked down and stared vacantly as Mama moved on to slicing tomatoes. Mama shaved them into the most perfect disks that you can imagine, a tough job considering how slimy tomatoes can be even without being bruised.

"Are you still planning on opening a restaurant someday?" Shawna asked, watching her.

Mama stopped slicing and stared out of the back window like she could imagine a world beyond Uncertain. "I'll have to keep on waiting and seeing."

There was a lot do tonight—like discuss the day's discoveries and make new plans, but Mama needed her spirits lifted urgently. There was one thing that usually did the trick. "Want to do an audition take for FoodieLand after we eat? It'll help me to test out my new camera."

"That's sweet of you to offer, but you have a guest. I'm sure you two have a lot of catching up to do," Mama said, smiling at Shawna.

If she only knew how hard I'd tried to do this earlier without getting too far.

Before Mama could make any more excuses, Shawna told her it would be fun. It's not like we could do much else with half of our team missing anyway. Where in the world were Emmett and Tim?

I hadn't realized how hungry I was until I spread some cream cheese on a thick slice of sourdough bread and layered veggies on top. I gobbled up my open faced sandwich in three bites, and I think Shawna ate hers in two.

Before the audition run, Shawna gave Mama a quick makeover and helped fluff up her hair. While Shawna overdid her own hair and makeup, she really brought out Mama's brown eyes with some pearly purple eye shadow and accentuated her high cheek bones with blush.

When we moved into the kitchen, I kept the camera as steady as possible as Mama put all those kitchen gadgets to work as she hammed it up in the kitchen, literally, by preparing a deviled ham, potato, and mushroom hash. "I dreamed this recipe up at work today," Mama said, "and these ingredients are what I had to work with."

"What inspires you, Chef Macy?" Shawna asked like she was the show hostess.

Mama stopped chopping onions to share how her mother, Gram, encouraged her to mix ingredients with love. "When I cook, it's for her and for those I adore." Mama turned to look right at the camera for full effect, but then I realized she wasn't being dramatic for the camera, she'd mentioned this for my sake.

Mama was a touch teary either from the burn of the onions or the conversation. "Do you know what my mother would've said right now?" Mama paused and then smiled. "Chuck Norris makes onions cry!"

It was one of Mama's best auditions ever, and it's like she knew it, too. She grabbed the camera from me and before I had a chance to edit anything, she scrolled through the pictures in an attempt to find the video I'd taken. Oops. Besides the other photos like the one of the dog caught midstream, she saw the close-up shot of the boar.

"How did you girls get this picture?" Mama asked, her voice tinged with alarm.

"We saw the pig off in the distance when we were climbing trees. That sure is some camera you bought Everdil for her birthday—the zoom feature is incredible."

Man, Shawna's dad must've taught her how to be a smooth talker like him this last year. I needed to take some lessons from her!

"Boars are dangerous," Mama said. "Both of you need to stay far, far away from them."

"Yes, ma'am," we said at the exact same time. Shawna and I exchanged a glance and put our hands over faces to keep our giggles from being so obvious.

12

Shawna, Mama, and I followed up our kitchen escapades by watching some back-to-back Garbage Can Gourmet competition episodes on FoodieLand. It was hard to focus on which contestants made the tastiest meal using pickled quail eggs, mustard, ghost peppers, and day old coffee grinds because I kept wondering why the heck Tim and Emmett hadn't come home yet. Mama called the marina during the commercial breaks, but no one answered.

"You think the boys are okay?" she asked.

I wondered the same thing, but there was no need to freak Mama out. "You know them—they probably just lost track of time."

A little before ten, the phone rang. I jumped up to answer it before Mama could. Shawna moved to the edge of the couch cushion as I answered, "Hey?"

"Hello there, Ms. Everdil," Mr. Nash said in that always professional way of his. "Do you happen to know Tim's whereabouts?"

"No, sir." Had I not recently seen Mr. Nash's underwear strewn about on the floor, I might've been a little more intimidated right then. I was telling the truth, though. Of course I couldn't share *everything* I knew because that would be breaking the rules that I myself swore we were no longer going to break. Yes, Emmett and Tim were home later than usual, but this didn't exactly constitute an emergency, at least not yet. I cleared my throat to sound calm as I spoke. "Emmett and Tim left here late this afternoon to go on a bike ride ... for fun, you know. I'm sure everything is fine."

Just as Shawna accused me of looking guilty earlier, her eyes were wide, and she looked on the cusp of another gasp.

"I'm not overly concerned but wanted to check in," Mr. Nash said into the receiver, though he wasn't too convincing. He paused for a moment as if I might offer up more information. Truly, I didn't know much else.

"Well, please call me if Tim shows up or as soon as you hear anything." Mr. Nash gave me his cell phone number and explained his plans to drive around the area looking for Emmett and Tim in case something wasn't right.

"I promise," I said, figuring I owed him that much for withholding a few minor details, emphasis on minor.

Once I hung up, I pictured the boys stranded in the woods, filthy and shivering. Maybe they'd been viciously attacked by a boar ... or worse. I cleared the image from my mind by imagining they had some exciting news to share with us that would lead to the prize of all prizes. Shawna searched for any information on her phone.

Mama called the marina again after I gave her a rundown of the conversation with Mr. Nash. Someone must've picked up this time. "Raleigh?" she said and then wasted no time before chewing Papa out. "Why haven't you answered? Any news on the boys?"

Both Shawna and I leaned in closer to Mama to see if we could overhear anything. All I could make out was the deep tone of Papa's voice rather than specific words.

"Fine then. Uh huh. Hmm. And you didn't think to call me right away? You're on a real roll, Raleigh," Mama said. Before the phone call ended, she added, "And don't expect me to fix you anything to eat when you get home, whenever that will be!"

Despite what she'd said, Mama had already made him a plate of the deviled ham, potato, and mushroom hash along with one for Emmett.

Shawna scrunched her face in concern, but I shrugged as if the tension between my parents was something new to me.

Mama sighed before sharing, "Gramps is driving Emmett and Tim home now. I guess something's wrong with Tim's bike."

"Do you know what happened?" Shawna asked.

Mama lifted her hands up in the air as if completely clueless. "Same type of shenanigans that you girls were up to earlier if I had to guess."

I stifled another laugh, especially since Mama was spot on

and I was so relieved that Emmett and Tim were okay.

True to my word earlier, I called Mr. Nash. His voice sounded much less uptight. "Thanks for the update, Ms. Everdil. I'll be arriving in approximately five minutes to pick Tim up."

I watched the clock, and sure enough, Mr. Nash arrived nearly three hundred seconds later, exactly when he said he would. While we waited for the boys to get here, Mama offered Mr. Nash some of the dish she'd prepared earlier, possibly Papa's portion.

Mr. Nash refused at first, but he caved in a moment later, probably because of the smell of caramelized onion still lingering in the house. He sat down, and once he shoveled in a big bite, he said, "This is amazing, Macy. Have you ever considered catering?"

Talking with a mouth full of food is one of Mama's pet peeves, but she didn't seem to mind too much given the ways her eyes sparkled a little brighter from his compliment.

"Mama's going to open a restaurant someday," I answered for her, hoping this would somehow make her feel more accountable for her dream.

"We'll see," Mama said, looking out the window again.

We'll see. I really disliked that phrase.

We watched on as Mr. Nash nearly licked his plate clean, and the moment he set his fork down, he said, "I always have a party at my house to kick off the Bigfoot Conference in the fall, and I'd love for you to consider catering it."

"Thank you," Mama said. "Maybe I will."

"Maybe I will" was a major improvement over "we'll see." And the fact that she was considering catering an event connected to such a thing as a Bigfoot conference showed that she might've been coming around.

Shawna dared to ask, "So, have there been any Bigfoot sightings in the park recently?"

I'd been so unprepared for her to bring up the forbidden topic that I choked on my own spit.

Mr. Nash jumped up and was about ready to do the Heimlich maneuver, but I managed to croak out, "I'm okay."

Mama brought me some water as Mr. Nash explained, "Only vocalizations."

"Vocalizations?" Shawna asked.

"Strange sounds that I've been able to capture on recordings." Mr. Nash went as far as mimicking some of the whistles, growls, and knocking noises he'd heard.

Mama raised an eyebrow, and I wondered if it was because she felt embarrassed for Mr. Nash like I kind of did or because she'd recalled the knocking noises we'd heard the night of the crash. If I had to bet, it was probably a combo of both.

Shawna *really* did have a future as a reporter given the way she asked her next question. "I see. So what is it that makes you believe in Bigfoot?"

Mr. Nash took his glasses with the thick lenses off before he responded. His eyes instantly looked smaller. "When I was about five years old, I went out swimming in the Caddo, alone. I hadn't realized how far I'd gone out until it was too late. I dunked under and struggled to come up for air several times before a fuzzy ape-like angel rescued me. It could've been an oxygen-deprived hallucination, but there's no way I would've gotten out of the lake alive given the state I was in. I became obsessed with apes and Bigfoot after that, making it my goal to protect the creature I believe saved me."

For someone who has a thing against talking with full mouths, I was surprised to see Mama staring at Mr. Nash with her mouth hanging wide open. Tim had told us the story before, but she was obviously hearing it for the first time.

Mr. Nash smiled and then put his glasses back on, his eyes back to their familiar size. "I know it sounds crazy, and I've received enough ridicule to make me want to recant, but I know in my heart what happened. And if a primate expert like Jane Goodall can believe in Bigfoot, then I might not be too off base." Mr. Nash then turned the "interview" around on Shawna. "Why all the cryptid interest?"

I almost started choking again when Shawna answered, "Because of the Bigfoot contest, of course. I think a lot of people are interested now. We saw someone at the grocery store who looked like he was a serious hunter. Well, minus a missing finger."

Mr. Nash shook his head as if in disbelief. "If it is the hunter I'm thinking of, he's bad news."

Approaching headlights lit up the living room. I exhaled now that Gramps arrived with Tim and Emmett safe and sound. I hadn't realized I'd been holding my breath.

True to my imagination, the boys were filthy. They weren't shivering, but they were sweaty and reeked as much as the gunk Shawna stepped in earlier. Just like us, the boys were scratched up. Tim had one heck of a purplish welt on the back of his hand, plus a huge scratch ran along the side of his cheek. Other than scrapes, Emmett didn't seem as injured, though he walked with a noticeable limp.

"Where were you? What happened?" Mama returned to nurse mode, fussing over my brother's scratches and his limp.

"I'm fine. Just pulled a muscle," Emmett said, practically brushing her off. He was acting tough to avoid looking like a wimp in front of his friends, especially Shawna. Otherwise, I can guarantee you he would've played up his injuries in an attempt to get more attention.

Tim stood a couple of inches taller than his dad now. Mr. Nash had to look up at his son to chew him out. "I would've appreciated a note or phone call at the very least!"

Gramps must've thought Mr. Nash was talking to him because he answered, "Sorry. Raleigh and I should've called right way to let you know these guys were safe with us."

"My apologies," Mr. Nash said, turning to Gramps. "I wasn't implying you should've called. Tim knows he should be more courteous and aware of his responsibilities. He'll spend the next twenty-four hours thinking about this while he's grounded."

Tim looked at the top of Mr. Nash's head as he answered, "Yes, sir. I didn't mean to upset you. I hit a hole that flattened my tire and warped the rim, and then it took us a while to walk to the marina to find a ride home."

"Raleigh and I spent a while trying to fix the tire, though it needs more work than what we had time for. The boys were antsy to get back," Gramps said as if that might change Mr. Nash's mind about the grounding business.

Mr. Nash shook Gramps' hand. "Thanks for looking out for Tim." He tried to shake Mama's hand next, but she wouldn't settle for that and put an arm around him. He nearly punched her shoulder as he readjusted and then apologized, but Mama laughed the hug mishap off.

"I'm glad Tim has such kind-hearted folks who are like family to him," Mr. Nash said. "Thanks for the hospitality, Macy."

I brainstormed what I could say or do to make Mr. Nash stay longer so Team Bigfoot would get a chance to talk, but there's no way we'd get any privacy with all these adults around. Our conversation would have to wait.

"See you soon," I told Tim before he left.

"Yeah, after I've done my time," he said in a low voice, but not low enough because his dad overheard him.

"Done your time *and* fixed your bike," Mr. Nash added with no trace of sympathy in his voice.

"Yes, sir," Tim said, back to looking at the ground.

Shawna swooped in to give Tim a hug that I would've never been brave enough to attempt. "Take care, Timmy."

I wonder if Tim saw me roll my eyes as he walked outside

with his dad.

Gramps helped transfer Tim's mangled bike from his cramped trunk to Mr. Nash's bike rack and then whispered something to Emmett before waving goodbye at the rest of us.

I was dying to know everything that had happened.

After Mr. Nash and Gramps left, Mama pulled Emmett's dinner plate out of the fridge. "I suppose I should ground you for the next day, too," she said, just about to microwave his food.

Emmett hadn't broken curfew or committed any real crime other than causing worry, but I bet Mama felt like she needed to keep up with Mr. Nash's stricter style of parenting.

Emmett could've easily sweet-talked his way out of being grounded, but to my surprise, his body sagged like he was relieved. "I understand, Mama, and dinner sure smells good, but I better go clean up," he said. And with that, he turned around and limped down the hallway to the bathroom.

Mama shook her head. "That's not like your brother at all."

It was even more unlike him when he started drawing a bath instead of showering. I wanted to run after Emmett and shake answers from him, but I needed to be more patient. If you can't tell by now, patience is not my strongest virtue.

13

Mama insisted Shawna should get to sleep in my bed since she was a guest, and she helped make me a pallet on the floor instead. I was too drained to really care. Emmett must've been even more exhausted because he went to sleep soon after taking a long bath. The bathroom was downright tropical when Shawna and I got ready for bed.

"You think he's okay?" Shawna asked.

"Yeah, his injuries seem minor enough."

Shawna caught me staring as she washed the makeup off her face. "I can teach you how to wear makeup if you're interested. Eyeliner is tricky. A couple of my friends and I did a blindfolded makeover at a sleepover. It was hilarious. We could try that sometime, too."

"Yeah, sure," I said even though a blindfolded makeover wasn't my idea of fun. Maybe I needed to be a teenager to understand.

Without her makeup on, Shawna looked younger and more like the girl I'd been friends with last year. I'm sure I looked exactly the same to her with my big frizzy hair and teeth that overlapped.

When daydreaming about having a slumber party with Shawna after she moved, I'd imagined how we would've chatted into the early morning hours. We'd remember stories like how we couldn't get each other's names right when we first met, and then we'd laugh at how someone with a last name of Minnoe could be so clueless about fishing. The first time she joined my family on a fishing trip, she shot a chunk of garlic cheese at Emmett's face when she casted her own line. Shortly after I'd won a stuffed fish out of one of those crane machines, I gave it to her, which is how Minnoe the Minnow came to be.

To top off my imaginary slumber party, Shawna would've said that she made new friends, but no one compared to Emmett, Tim, and especially not to ME.

Our actual slumber party was nothing of the sort. She tossed one of my favorite stuffed animals aside and said, "I'm so over pigs!" Instead of a heart-to-heart chat like I'd wanted, Shawna spent time talking to both of her parents and then tinkered around with her cell phone like it held the secrets to the universe.

The stress of the day and all that worrying and wondering caught up with me, and as I started to nod off, Shawna whispered, "Hey, Everdil, do you believe Mr. Nash?"

Sure, Mr. Nash's story sounded far-fetched, but I answered, "Why would he lie about it? And why would you dare mention the contest to him?"

"If we bring the contest right out in the open, we look more innocent that way," she explained. Was this something she'd learned from her lawyer dad or from hanging around big city kids?

"You ever miss Uncertain?"

"Just my family, I guess." Sadness seeped into her voice. "Dad said he's looking forward to me coming home, but my mom will probably need some help with my grandma."

"What do you want to do?"

Shawna was so quiet I thought she might've fallen asleep. "I don't know. Dad gets so busy sometimes he barely knows I exist, and now Mom has her hands full taking care of my grandma."

"I'm sure your Dallas friends would miss you, especially since you're so popular and all, but you have friends here, too."

"Yeah," she said half-heartedly. "I'm exhausted, and my head's starting to hurt. Goodnight, Everdil."

I rolled over. When had I stopped being enough of a friend for her? I was so zonked that I didn't dwell on it for long and had dreams about the boar and smashed bikes.

When I woke up, the sun had another hour or so before it would rise. Shawna was still sleeping, and I totally had to take a picture of her. Her face was mashed into my pillow, making her lips pucker out all fish-Minnoe-like. She must've tossed and turned a lot because my favorite set of sheets had somehow wrapped around her legs mummy-style. I wondered if "Timmy" would find this picture as funny as I did.

I took another photo and thought the camera made a weird clicking noise, but it was Emmett at the door. "You awake, Everdil?" he whispered.

I opened the door so swiftly that Emmett almost knocked on my forehead. I held my finger to my lips and pointed to Shawna as I escorted him into my room. Emmett took one look at Shawna and snickered. For as sound as she'd been sleeping, Shawna rolled to her side, winding the sheets even tighter around her legs. Her eyes popped open, and she attempted to sit up but was too caught up in the fabric to move.

Emmett started laughing even harder now, and as quiet as I'd tried to be, I lost it.

"What's so funny?" Shawna asked, pulling her burgundy streaked hair over her face as if she was trying to cover a giant zit.

You probably had to be there, but when she asked this, we both laughed even harder. It's a wonder we didn't wake Mama and Papa up.

Shawna kicked off the sheets, and I finally stopped laughing when I heard the sound of fabric ripping. Have I mentioned those were my favorite sheets? Gram had given the set to me when I was a little girl.

"Sorry," she said, like it was no big deal. Yeah, for her it was no big deal, but stuff like this couldn't be replaced. Shawna sat on the edge of the bed, straightening out her owl-patterned jammies since they'd gotten twisted too. "Seriously, why are you guys laughing at me? Do I look bad?"

"No, you look … pretty," Emmett said, but he must've been nervous because the word "pretty" came out sounding like "purdy."

My case of the giggles continued, but I was the only one laughing now. I cleared my throat and tried to act more serious. "You do look pretty," I said, accentuating the last part of the word to sound less hick. "Especially without the paint on your face."

Shawna crossed her arms as if I'd offended her.

"I didn't mean it like that. Anyway, we're wasting time," I said to move things along. "We've been dying to know what happened, Emmett."

My brother sat down at my desk and winced. "First, Tim and I found this really weird pine tree close to Swamp Sam's cabin. The trunk was twisted like massive hands had bent it in half. When we were checking out the area for other suspicious signs, we came across a huge hog trap. As we got a closer look, Swamp Sam snuck up on us and said, 'Leave, spies, or I'll shoot!'

"I hollered out that I was Raleigh's boy, but Swamp Sam didn't hear me or didn't care because the next thing we knew, he pulled a shotgun on us. Right as I jumped on my bike to get away, I felt a blast of pain. Tim got hit on his hand, and something grazed his face. We managed to get on our bikes and pedaled for our lives, and that's when Tim ran his bike into a hole. I dragged him out of the area before Swamp Sam could shoot us to smithereens."

Swamp Sam had issues, but how could he shoot at two kids? Two kids he knew at that!

"Do you need to go to the hospital?" Shawna asked.

Emmett's face got all blotchy like he was having an allergic reaction again. "Gramps did more than try to fix Tim's bike. He recognized right away that we'd been blasted with rock salt instead of real bullets and told me that if I soaked in a bath for a while, it would help take the sting of the rock salt away. It still hurts this morning but not anything like yesterday."

So that explains the limp and the long bath. As I continued thinking this over, Shawna surprised me by catching the laughing bug next. "Did you get shot in the butt?"

Emmett stayed silent which meant she was right! He didn't find this one bit funny, but I sure did.

"Hey, I was risking my life for the cause while you girls were shopping." He drew the word "girls" out like an insult.

Shawna calmed down and told him about the boar attack. And in case the seriousness of her tale didn't sink in, I showed him the picture.

"Whoa—that thing is mammoth!" Emmett said. He looked at Shawna all sensitively now. "Are you okay?"

She nodded.

"I'm fine, too, in case you were wondering," I told Emmett. "You're not the only one risking your life. Or busting your butt." Shawna and I cracked up over this.

"I guess you don't care to hear the rest of what I had to say then," Emmett said, standing up and walking his way slowly out of my room. His limp wasn't as pronounced.

"Stop!" Shawna said.

He was toying with us, but I wanted to know what he was referring to just as badly as Shawna. "We'll quit giving you a hard time, okay?"

Emmett nodded, knowing he had accomplished exactly what he wanted. "Gramps lied. Papa wasn't helping me and Tim—he was doing a deal with some guy at the marina. I overheard the guy offer Papa a job to privately charter one of the pontoons."

"Let me guess, did the guy resemble George Washington dressed up for a safari, only without the wig and one middle finger?" I asked.

"How did you know?"

"Everdil saw him at the grocery store, and he's the one who led us to the boar," Shawna explained.

"Mr. Nash said he's bad news. We have to tell Papa he can't take the job."

"He already did. I couldn't sleep well last night and heard Papa when he came home late. Mama was miffed until he told her about the job. The guy obviously offered a lot of money."

I heaved a sigh. There was no way Papa would turn down a

well-paying job. Maybe Mama would make him reconsider given what Mr. Nash said, but then I thought about the bills and the bank calling. Even if the hunter was bad news and complicated matters, we needed the cash. And really, what were the odds of any of us winning the contest?

Not impossible, I told myself considering the recent happenings. "We should keep tabs on what Papa and this guy are up to," I said. "Maybe they'll unknowingly lead us to a discovery like before."

"Maybe," Emmett said. "I'll research as much as I can today while I rest up."

"You mean while you're grounded," I said, and Emmett grinned.

"Want to go shopping today while the boys are out of commission?" Shawna asked me.

I'm not into shopping, especially since I never have the money to buy much, but we needed some supplies if we were going to take things to the next level.

"So what's for breakfast, Emmett? Are you going to make crepes again, or do you want to garbage-can breakfast for us with some other ingredients?"

Emmett shrugged as he answered, "Cereal."

"Oh," Shawna said. "You don't cook anymore? I always thought you'd own your own restaurant someday like your mom wants to."

Emmett smiled, probably because she'd remembered he could cook, and then he cut the pretense. "I've gotten even better since you moved. I'll make us crepes, but just like you both promised not to give me a hard time about getting shot in the bu—backside, you better not give me a hard time about my cooking."

I tell you what—it took some serious inner strength to not laugh. One thing that helped me keep it together was the idea that the contest deadline was now seven days away.

14

Mama and Papa had woken up a short while after the three of us had our secret meeting and joined us for breakfast. Too bad we didn't have cream cheese frosting to swipe since Emmett had pitched the rest of the cake.

Just as the crepes were light and airy, so was the mood as we sat around the table. Mama and Papa held hands while we said grace, and they stayed connected even after our group "Amen." Emmett gawked at them while serving a plate of chopped fruit. It had been a long time since we'd seen them hold hands like that.

"I think this is one of the best things I've ever eaten," Shawna said after her first bite of breakfast.

"I could've made the crepe batter a little thinner," Emmett said, almost like he was begging for her to continue to praise his culinary greatness.

He didn't get that chance because Mama cleared her throat and made a funny face at Shawna. "What am I, chopped liver?"

"I mean, except for everything that you've prepared, Mrs. Jackson." Shawna had eased up on the makeup this morning, and her cheeks naturally blushed now.

"I'm just giving you a hard time, Shawna. I'll take it is a compliment as I've trained Emmett myself," Mama said with a laugh. "And chopped liver. Now there's an idea for a future meal."

"Mom!" Emmett said in a whiny voice.

Papa laughed a deep laugh—a sound I realized I'd missed hearing just like I'd missed seeing Mama and Papa show affection. "I've got some good news," he announced.

I knew what he was talking about but acted clueless when I asked, "What?"

"I took on a nice private charter at the marina," he said with a smile like he was proud of himself. Once again, he had something stuck between his teeth. I passed him a napkin, but he didn't get the hint. He balled it up in his hand. "I hope you'll be extra helpful for Mama's sake since I'll be gone a lot the next week or so."

I wanted to point out that he'd been gone an awful lot already as it was, but kept this to myself. "Congrats, but is the job safe?"

"Thanks for looking out for me as well as your mom, Everdil, but every job has its share of risks. You never know if a pontoon might go off course after someone spies Bigfoot." Papa winked at me.

"Ha ha!" I said, not finding his comment the least bit funny as everyone else at the table. "Seriously, though ..."

"I signed a confidentiality agreement and can't share the details about my new client, but rest assured I'll be as safe as possible."

No doubt Papa meant to be reassuring, but the "as possible" part got to me. I hated the thought of that man putting him in danger. That's when I got an idea. "Will Gramps take over the tours then while you're busy? Shawna wants to go on one real bad while she's in town."

Shawna shot me a questioning look but went along with things even though she'd said nothing of the sort.

"I'm sure Gramps would love that," Papa said.

Yes! I had a feeling this might lead to something big.

"I've got some good news too," Mama said, catching me completely off guard.

"Did FoodieLand call?" Emmett asked, nearly falling out of his chair.

Mama's expression flattened when she answered, "No, but since things are looking up with your father's new opportunity, I took the day off since I've been putting in so many hours."

It had been ages since she'd had a day off. While I wanted to explore and find answers, this could work to our advantage. "Great, Mama. Shawna and I were thinking of going shopping—"

I didn't have a chance to finish my sentence because Mama was all over a shopping trip the way flies flock to you-know-what. We said goodbye to Papa and Emmett, and then we were out the door in a matter of minutes. I sure hoped my brother would find out some useful information while we were gone besides resting his behind.

We headed to Marshall, which was only about a half an hour away. I've always loved going there, and around Christmastime, Gram and Gramps used to take me and Emmett to walk the twinkling Wonderland of Lights display. I sure missed Gram, and this made me think of Shawna's family. "Any update on your grandma?"

"She's about the same, maybe even more out of it based on Mom's latest report."

"Oh," I said, hoping for better news. "Maybe we could buy her some cookies or something today."

Mama looked at me in the review mirror with pride as she responded, "That's a great idea, Everdil."

Then I was thrown forward when she slammed on the brakes, the seatbelt digging into my stomach and shoulder.

"You girls okay?" Mama asked before I could figure out what had happened.

"Fine," I answered. "Geez, you would've thought Bigfoot jumped in front of the car."

Shawna massaged her collarbone while Mama placed a hand over her heart. A deer stood in the middle of the road in broad daylight with its eyes so wide that it looked possessed or rabid. It was only a few feet away from being roadkill. It was large enough that our car probably would've been roadkill, too.

Mama laid on the horn, but the deer didn't budge. It gazed *through* us in the most haunted of ways until the sound of a shotgun rang out in the distance. Well, that explained things. Hunting season was over, but some folks around here believed they should be able to kill anything whenever they wanted, at least according to Papa's grumblings.

"Dang poacher," Mama said under her breath as she drove off now that the deer had sprinted into the woods. "I want you girls to be extra careful when you play outside."

She made it sound like we were little kids, but at least she didn't make plans to supervise us like she had done after a nearby hiker got accidentally shot by a poacher a few years back. I thought we'd never hear the end of that incident.

We settled on going to the large superstore since it would have everything we needed. The aisles were bright and so was our conversation as the three of us poked through the clothing section, probably since we realized how lucky we'd been to avoid a major accident.

15

"This would look good on you," Shawna said, holding up a dress from the junior's section that was turquoise—my favorite color. She'd remembered.

"You're right, Shawna." Mama had been trying to get me to wear dresses for a while, and I sometimes did, just on rare church occasions.

The dress had sequins around the collar that made it look pretty but not over-the-top-girlie. I wondered what Tim would think about it. I shook my head and explained, "It isn't practical." I hoped Shawna would interpret "practical" as "this won't work for Team Bigfoot."

Mama tossed the dress in the cart to "try on at least" as we helped find Shawna some clothes that would work for the team, not like we let Mama in on that fact.

"Cute, you'll be like twinsies again," Mama said as Shawna picked out some camouflage shorts and a coordinating tan tank. It seemed like forever ago when we used to dress similarly. Shawna stopped for a moment like she was re-thinking this, but then she tossed the outfit into the cart anyway.

It would take a whole lot more than an outfit for us to be twinsies. I exhaled. "Let's try this on so we can look at other stuff."

In the fitting room, Shawna posed in front of the mirror like she was bound for a fashion shoot rather than traipsing around in the woods hunting a cryptid. And when I tried the dress on, well, there really was nothing practical about it.

"You actually look pretty," Shawna said. I know she likely meant it as a compliment, but it sure didn't sound like one.

"You do," Mama agreed, which hurt my feelings just as much since she seemed oblivious to Shawna's insult/compliment.

"We've got other things we should be buying," I said, ready to change out of the dress and set it back on the rack.

Mama insisted that I get it, though. "You'd shock everyone with how great you look," she said. I admit this got to me, as I wouldn't mind shocking one person in particular.

As if that wasn't enough, Mama added, "Your dad just got paid, and the dress doesn't cost much."

Without thinking that Shawna was standing right there, I blurted out, "But what about the bank calling?"

"We're getting it straightened out," Mama said, setting the

dress back in the cart, this time like it was for keeps. "That's for us to worry about, not you."

I did worry though, even if I decided to get the dress anyway. One piece of clothing wasn't a huge deal with everything else considered.

Shawna put the clothes she wanted in the cart, and then we split from Mama while she picked out some groceries.

"You should get some blue cheese and bologna for a practice run," I told her.

"That's not a bad idea." Mama took the cart with her, tucking the dress in the back like she wanted to keep me from changing my mind.

"Things have been rough lately for your family, huh?" Shawna said as we made our way to the outdoor section.

I shrugged. "It would be great if my parents were rich like yours or if we could hurry up and win this contest."

Shawna laughed, but it sounded forced. "Money won't fix everything. It doesn't buy time, and it won't make you well."

That seemed like something Gramps would say. A million dollars couldn't bring Gram back.

We were passing by the home décor section when Shawna stopped and changed the subject. "You should consider redecorating your room." She flipped through a poster display full of boy band pictures and some with wild designs.

Posters weren't my style, but I'd been thinking about painting over the busy floral wallpaper. Maybe the dress gave me some confidence and so did these conversations. The truth is I kind of wanted to reinvent myself too, only without all that makeup. "You're right." I grabbed a nearby abandoned cart and Shawna helped me select a drum of buttercream paint as well as a few painting supplies. The color looked soft and calm and yummy. Plus, it had a touch of gold to remind me of the chain around my neck and the sunshine outside.

As we continued through the superstore, we passed a section of shotguns and BB guns and more serious weapons locked up. Shawna turned her attention to pocketknives on the shelf. Some of them were puny and would offer no defense against massive Bigfoot fangs, or boars.

Shawna's nowhere near as clumsy as I am, but she knocked several packages off of the shelf. When I bent down to help her pick them up, I couldn't believe it when I saw her slip the smallest of knives into her pocket.

A pocketknife is not the type of thing you need to "try on."

"What are you doing?" I asked, wanting what I saw to be nothing more than a misunderstanding.

"Shh," she said, glancing around as she set the other knives back in place.

This was no misunderstanding. "Put it back, or I'm telling."

"Don't be such a little kid about this, Everdil."

"Your popular friends in Dallas might go around stealing stuff, but that's not right."

"Look Everdil, they're not going to let a kid buy a knife, and we'll have more money to spend on other things this way."

"It's wrong. A thief doesn't belong on our team. I'm sure Emmett and Tim will agree with me." And if they didn't? Well, I'd venture out solo. Skewing the truth was one thing, but stealing was breaking one of the commandments. Shawna could do whatever she wanted, but I wasn't going down with her.

I was on the verge of tears as I walked off. I hate the fact that I sometimes cry when I get angry. I guess I expected Shawna to come running after me repenting of her ways.

I even stopped and picked up a cheap compass and a flashlight with a carabiner to give her some extra time to change her mind. Nothing, which made me start to worry about the things in my room she might try to pocket, like my necklace. I wasn't going to take it off again with her around.

I put the flashlight back and set out to find Mama, but I stopped when a man raised his voice near the gun counter. At first I thought it was because Shawna had gotten busted, but then someone responded, "I can't sell you a gun, sir. There's a protocol in Texas."

"Forget the protocol! I'm trying to protect people from a takeover!" I knew the voice—Swamp Sam.

I rounded the corner and saw him standing by the case. He

had a few new sores on his face, and his skin was peeling. He must've dropped more weight the way his hunting attire sagged.

The guy behind the gun counter crossed his arms. "Sir, please calm down. If you refuse to fill out the background check, I can't sell you a gun. It's as simple as that."

"I have the right to bear arms! And I already own several guns, you idiot. I just need a new rifle."

"I'm sorry, sir."

Swamp Sam pounded on the glass gun case. "You don't understand! Bigfoot is building an army to destroy us, with the government's help mind you, and I need to fire out warnings to keep that from happening!"

The guy talked into a walkie-talkie and requested immediate back-up. Swamp Sam must've gotten the hint because he stepped away. "You're making things worse by not selling me the gun," he said before walking off. The guy let out a nervous chuckle and said something else into his walkie-talkie, but I couldn't quite hear.

As I set out to find Mama, I listened for sirens and watched for police officers rushing through the store to arrest Swamp Sam, or maybe even Shawna for shoplifting. Before I reached the grocery section, a hand reached for my shoulder, and I about yelped thinking it was a store employee sent to interrogate me.

"I put the knife back," Shawna said, holding onto a pair of binoculars. "Did you hear what just happened?"

"That was Swamp Sam talking crazy," I said.

"At first I thought it was some kind of made-for-TV prank,

but Swamp Sam was serious about the Bigfoot and government conspiracy stuff, wasn't he?" she said. When I didn't respond, she asked, "Hey, are we cool?"

I eyed her pocket to see if it had a knife-shaped lump.

"Seriously. I put it back." Shawna patted her pocket for good measure.

"I still plan on telling the boys, and I should tell my parents plus yours."

Shawna kicked at a scuff mark on the ground. "Like my parents would even care with everything they have going on, but do you have to tell the others? I didn't *actually* steal anything."

She made a good point. "I guess."

We met up with Mama, and she asked if we'd heard that Swamp Sam was in the store causing trouble. Funny how quickly news can spread wherever you are, small town or a superstore.

"He didn't look so well, and he seems to be losing it," I said.

"How incredibly sad," Mama said. "He's an intelligent man, but Papa said he's been refusing help. I should bring him some food," she said, investigating the paint and the supplies in my cart before we headed to the checkout lanes. "What's all this for?"

"Shawna and I were thinking about redecorating my room—is that okay?"

Mama hesitated for a moment. "I'll miss those sweet flowers, but I guess it's time for a fresh look, huh?"

Shawna and I helped put Mama's items, including the dress, on the belt at the checkout line. I flinched at how much everything cost, and when Mama swiped her credit card, the register printed out a small piece of paper.

The cashier glanced at the paper with a look of concern and pity. "Seems like the payment didn't go through. Could be a technical issue, like the satellite connection or something," the cashier said in a much-too-cheerful manner. She swiped the card again, but we all knew it wasn't some technical issue or some satellite in the atmosphere acting wonky. "Do you have another way of paying for this?" the cashier asked.

Mama's voice choked. "No, I'm sorry."

The cashier gave us another look of concern and pity until Shawna piped up, "Actually, we have cash. Can you add these other items to the total?" She handed her items over and then paid nearly two hundred dollars before Mama could refuse.

"Wonderful!" the cashier said with a phony smile.

As soon as we were out of earshot of the cashier, Mama thanked Shawna and told her she'd pay her back immediately.

"My parents gave me the money since they didn't want me to be a burden on your family while I'm staying with you guys," Shawna said. "They'll be upset if you don't accept it. Please."

I'm not sure how much of this was truthful, but Mama thanked her several times, and I took her aside to say, "That was incredibly generous."

"It was nothing."

"Thanks. I'm sorry I doubted you earlier, Shawna Minnoe."

16

Like the gentleman he normally wasn't, Emmett carried the bags inside once we got home. He even helped unpack and when he saw the neatly folded dress in a bag, he told Shawna, "That's nice."

"It's for your sister," Shawna said, keeping it a secret that she'd bought all this stuff with her very own money. I promised to keep her near-shoplifting secret in return.

I thought Emmett was about to say something mean, but all he said was, "Hmmm."

"Care to help me make some apple rhubarb popovers?" Mama asked Emmett, probably to keep the two of us from getting into a fight. She might've just been eager to whip up something tasty with her sous chef on her day off.

"Considering I'm grounded, do I have much of a choice?" Emmett asked.

Mama laughed. "Well, you can help the girls redecorate Everdil's room instead. Your choice."

Emmett chose the popovers, but he carried the paint to the room for us. He wasn't merely trying to impress Shawna—he had news.

He partially closed the door. "So I found out Swamp Sam's real name is Samuel Blinn. There's not much info on him, but he's lived in East Texas all his life, and he graduated from Jefferson High School. The only real thing of interest is that he had an arrest record from several years ago for misconduct with a weapon, but I couldn't find any details."

Misconduct with a weapon? Made sense as to why he'd refuse the background check, and it wasn't surprising for someone who shot two boys with rock salt (never mind the fact they were trespassing). We told him about what happened at the store.

"I doubt he'll be getting a new gun any time soon," Emmett said and gave us more info. "Tim looked into the hunter. I guess he's some big shot politician from Dallas named Dierk Robinson."

"It makes sense why he looks familiar now. I've seen him on the news," Shawna said, stopping to check out some things on her phone.

While she researched, Emmett helped me move my furniture out of the way.

After a few minutes, Shawna showed us a mug shot that looked exactly like the man we'd seen at the store, only more haggard. "This guy has been in trouble with the law, too. I guess he voted for stricter gun control laws but then got busted for shooting a rhino on an animal preserve. Not only that, but it was with some high-powered illegal rifle."

"Why would anyone shoot a rhino?" I asked, remembering the black rhinoceros we'd seen at the Houston zoo when we went there on a family trip. Tim had gone with us, listing facts about each animal like how the rhinoceros was endangered. The zoo trip had been ages ago, but I clearly remembered the rhino's size and the majestic way it roamed around. I also remembered a beautiful female gorilla nursing a newborn baby, though the boys seemed less impressed because it didn't pee about eight gallons like the rhino did.

Emmett shrugged again. "Why would someone want to shoot Bigfoot? That's my guess why he's here."

Shawna read more from the article. "Anyway, his lawyer got him off the hook somehow by claiming that Dierk shot the rhino out of self-defense. He supposedly lost his finger in that incident. You think the rhino nipped it off?"

"I doubt the rhino mistook his finger for a carrot," Emmett said.

Well, now Dierk's safari outfit made more sense. It sickened me to think of him hunting endangered creatures. For what reason? The thrill of the kill? I closed my eyes to say a prayer for Papa's safety, especially if Dierk had some illegal weapons on him now. My prayer was interrupted by the sound of a loud rip.

Shawna held a huge chunk of wallpaper in her hand. "Sorry, I couldn't help myself."

Now that my few pieces of furniture were out of the way, Emmett said he'd check back in later. I'd planned on painting over the wallpaper, but Shawna continued ripping off sections. I could see why. There was something so satisfying about tearing chunks of it off the wall.

Using her nails to dig at a large piece, Shawna tugged. "This is for cruel people like Dierk," she said. *Rip!*

I followed Shawna's lead, using the semi-sharp edge of a pair of scissors to remove the wallpaper behind my desk. "And for Swamp Sam losing his mind!" *Rip!*

"For my grandmother having a stroke." *Rip!*

"For Gram dying." *Rip!*

"For my parents who are always too busy." *Rip!*

"For my parents and their money worries." *Rip!*

"For the kids at school who are mean to me." *Rip!*

I stopped demolishing the wallpaper for a moment, stunned to hear Shawna's confession. "Aren't you Miss Popular now?"

Shawna gave the wallpaper a rest. "Sure, I got invited to one sleepover, but I'm hardly Miss Popular. Not like you'd know, but it's hard to be the new kid at a big school. I'm an outsider there. At home with my dad, too."

"But you've always had me ..."

"The longer I went without talking to you, the more I didn't think I could. Your life has been moving on too, Everdil. I see what's going on between you and Tim."

"You're kidding, right?" I dug some of the sticky stuff from underneath my nails.

"I can tell you like him."

I didn't deny that I liked Tim, but I sure wasn't confirming it either. "He's more into you. You two are both teenagers, and you're the pretty one."

"You think?" After an awkward pause, she added, "You're pretty too, even if you don't always show it."

"Thanks, I suppose." I went back to work and took out another chunk of wallpaper. Even if things weren't the way I wanted them to be, Shawna was right—my life had been moving on, too. "For Shawna who I lost contact with, but who is here now." *Rip!*

We shared a small smile that reminded me of the old days.

The spicy smell of cinnamon drifted into the room by the time we finished.

"You're lucky," Shawna said, stretching out on my bed that now took over the center of the room. She made a point of inhaling loudly.

I flopped next to her to stretch out my back. Shawna might've been talking about the rich smells wafting from the kitchen, but I had a feeling she meant something deeper. "Yeah," I agreed, even if I don't always consider myself the luckiest of people. Winning the million dollars would change all that, of course.

Once I rested for a minute, I gathered the flowery shards of wallpaper into a ball. My room looked bigger since the walls were incredibly plain now. Before I dumped the wallpaper into a large trash bag, I studied the roses and the innocent pink color one last time. I no longer felt like the little girl who pretended to like it. There was a lump in my throat so big it kept me from swallowing for a moment.

Good thing that sensation didn't last for long because we had apple rhubarb popovers to devour.

When we walked into the kitchen, Emmett scooted behind Mama. No wonder—he sported Mama's frilly pink cupcake patterned apron. "Cupcake Cutie," the apron read.

"You almost look as pretty as your sister does in her new dress, Emmett," Shawna said.

"I thought so myself." Mama pointed to her apron. "There's no way I was going to let him wear this one when he's grounded." She was wearing the one Papa had given her for Christmas that said, "While I have this apron on, I'm the boss. Any questions?"

"What? Real men wear aprons," Emmett said.

"Sure," Shawna said, "aprons with cupcakes on them."

The popovers were tasty enough to win top prize at any county fair, and if the people at FoodieLand ever paid attention, they'd amaze the judges.

After our tasty snack and changing into Papa's ratty t-shirts, all four of us tackled the paint job. I hesitated to take off the necklace to keep paint from getting on it, but I wasn't too worried about Shawna nabbing it anymore.

I loved dipping the roller into the paint and spreading the cheerful buttercream color. The wall went from looking shabby to glistening new in a matter of a few strokes, of course with texture from some wallpaper pieces that wouldn't come off as well as the residue. Wet droplets of paint sprinkled my hand and arm.

Mama blasted the radio, singing along to an old song about how "these boots were made for walking" as she painted the opposite wall. Normally, this would've embarrassed me, but I set my roller down in the tray of paint and grabbed a handful of pencils off of my desk so she could use them as a pretend microphone. Even Emmett got into the music, two-stepping with a paint brush. Shawna laughed so hard she put her hand on her stomach like it hurt.

The only way I would've felt any luckier in that moment is if Tim, Gramps, and Papa could've been there, too. And Gram.

After we cleaned up, the paint smell in my room was heavy, so Mama diced an entire onion, set it in a bowl, and added some water. "Trust me, it'll take some of the paint smell away."

Go figure an onion could get rid of stink. Much stranger things had happened this summer.

"Chuck Norris would be making that onion cry right now, wouldn't he?" Shawna said when we set the bowl on my desk, obviously remembering what Mama had said during her audition.

"Just after he popped a wheelie on a unicycle," Emmett added.

We cracked up. Everything felt right at that moment though things were about to get more complicated.

17

Since the boys had properly served their time, I called Gramps to schedule our own private tour.

A deep voice answered the line at the marina. "Raleigh's Tours. This is Raleigh speaking. What kind of tour are you interested in?"

"Hi Papa, it's Everdil. Why aren't you showing Dierk around?"

"He gave me the morning off. Wait ... how do you know my client's name?"

I pretended to sneeze to give myself a moment to think of an appropriate cover. It wasn't the most original lie, but I said, "I thought you mentioned it. Anyway, is Gramps there?"

"Sure, hold on," Papa said, letting the Dierk thing slide.

"What's going on Everdil Pickle?" Gramps asked as soon as he came on the phone.

"Shawna's only here for a short time this summer and she really wants to go on a tour. I just happen to know the perfect tour guide ..."

"The perfect tour guide, huh?" Gramps asked. I could tell he was smiling. "You're talking to the guy who would do anything for his favorite granddaughter. How about a tour tomorrow afternoon?"

"Perfect. I love you, Gramps!"

"Back atcha, Everdil Pickle."

Since we'd have to wait until tomorrow for the boat tour, today would be perfect for the park. But first, Shawna wanted to stop by to see her mom and grandmother and bring something yummy like I'd mentioned. Emmett and I were on board, but they chose to whip up a fresh batch of popovers to bring instead of something packaged like what I had in mind.

"How can I help?" I asked.

"Don't cook anything," Emmett said. He proceeded to tell Shawna how I ruined eggs and once cooked a pot of rice that was somehow crunchier after I cooked it than before.

"Only Chuck Norris could do that," I said.

"No, he can cook minute rice in a second flat."

Just like the kitchen had warmed up both from the oven and the summer heat, Shawna seemed to have warmed up to Emmett as she stood close to him rolling out dough like she was his sous chef. I did dishes.

Mama was back at work, though it would've been nice to

have her around. We could've filmed an audition and tried to get Emmett on one of the shows, too. He'd learned his baking soda lesson and would be one heck of a competitor.

Tim showed up on time and kept his hand over his face, but he couldn't hide the shiner on his cheek. The bruise on his hand had deepened to a darker shade of purple.

While Shawna and Emmett set the popovers in the oven, he asked me, "Need some help?" Shawna glanced at my direction and gave me a knowing look, but I shook my head in denial.

"Fine then," Tim said, misunderstanding my head shake.

"No, you can help," I said, shoving a wet plate at him. He dropped it on the floor. A piece of the edge chipped off, but the plate was still functional … enough. "Sorry, Tim."

Emmett and Shawna thought this was hilarious. I focused on washing while Tim dried the dishes so I wouldn't have to look at any of them. By the time the popovers cooled off, so had I. This batch rivaled the ones from the day before.

"Great job, Shawna," Tim said with a plop of sticky apple filling stuck on his chin.

"Thanks," she responded, and for a moment I thought she was going to take full credit for baking the popovers, but she added, "this was Emmett's doing. I can't get over what a good cook he is."

Tim's eyes widened. "Emmett, you made these?"

Unless it came to our family, Emmett normally brushed off his love for cooking like crumbs from a messy coffee cake, but not this time. "Really. Shawna helped a lot, though."

I smiled at him and could almost picture my brother all grown up—he'd be buff and taller than Papa by that point, though not freakishly Bigfoot tall. He'd play football for the NFL, but he'd also run his own restaurant like that old guy, John Elway. I saw an episode about him and other stars who owned restaurants on FoodieLand. Okay, maybe that daydream was a stretch, but he had potential.

"You should've seen Emmett wearing his mom's cupcake apron," Shawna teased.

"Oh man, I missed that? You should wear that to football practice next season," Tim said.

"You're just jealous." Emmett play-tackled Tim.

Once the boys stopped roughhousing, Emmett placed the popovers on a paper plate and covered them in foil before loading them in his backpack.

Emmett carried the backpack so carefully you would've thought it was loaded with a baby inside, or a bomb. I suppose I carried my camera case the same way.

We'd borrowed Gramps' bike for Shawna to use, but she was so wobbly on it that I let her take mine instead. I kept my own helmet though, and somehow, Shawna managed to even look pretty with Gramps' bulky helmet protecting her skull. Tim looked goofy in his—the helmet mashed his shaggy hair onto his forehead. His legs were so long that his jeans were now an inch too short and looked even shorter when he sat on his bike.

"Expecting a flood?" I asked him. Served him right for teasing me after I tripped at his house a while back.

"No," he answered, but it came out like a squeak instead. He cleared his throat and said no again, and this time his voice sounded normal.

As we set off to Shawna's mom's house, I lagged behind. Gramps' bike peddles were stiff, and I had to use much more force to get the bike to move forward than I was used to. Plus the bike seat sat up higher as did the connecting bar.

Tim, Emmett, and Shawna sped on ahead, acting like chummy stooges who had no idea they were ditching the fourth.

"Wait up!" I called out, but they didn't hear me. Or worse, they didn't care. It wasn't long before they were completely out of sight.

As I rounded a bend on Old 134, a long and sharp whistle rang out, kind of the noise you might expect from a howler monkey at the zoo, only different and deeper. It echoed off of the road and the many surrounding trees. Emmett, Shawna, and Tim had to be messing with me.

"Ha ha!" I hollered. "You guys are funny!"

But then a knocking sound followed another whistle, like a rock being pounded against a tree trunk. It reminded me of the noises we heard the night of the birthday boat incident.

My skin prickled. Maybe this was something more than a practical joke. I stopped pedaling and wiped sweat from my face. Common sense told me to move along, but I pushed that part of my brain aside.

I'd check things out for a moment and then catch up to the

others. I knew where they were going and had a feeling they'd eventually come back for me. I maneuvered my bike off the road and rested it against a tree, hanging my helmet off the handlebars. The woods stretched on for miles and miles, so I waited for another whistle to determine which way to explore. The bizarre noise made me battle with common sense again.

After hesitating, I followed a trail created by some sort of off-road vehicle. I held the camera in my hand. The oils and the sweat from my palm left a film on the preview screen.

Papa had taught me to pay close attention to my surroundings to avoid getting lost on a hike, and that's exactly what I did as I made my way deeper into the woods. I mentally noted the location of a rotting log on the ground, a group of vines dangling from a branch, and a bird's nest way up in a tree. The trail curved to the left ahead, but a loud knocking noise emerged from the right.

The trail was convenient, but if I had a chance of spying Bigfoot, I needed to follow the sounds. I glanced around to memorize my location. A tree stood out that looked as though it had been split and charred by a bolt of lightning. I'd find it after checking things out and then would return to my bike and get on my merry way with hopefully a million-dollar worthy photograph.

A booming knock followed a short, shrill whistle. And then, BANG! The unmistakable sound of a gun. My heart pounded so hard it hurt. Is that how Gram felt before her heart attack?

A hunter had to be close. Had he bagged Bigfoot?

That common sense voice screamed for me to leave, but again I muted it to find out what had happened.

The brush was particularly thick to climb through, and after a while, I came upon a clearing with a tall deer blind and piles of corn scattered about. About forty feet or less away, a bloody body was sprawled out on the ground. It wasn't large enough to be Bigfoot, but what in the world was it?

I inched my way closer to get a better look. I knelt down so I could identify the dead animal as a deer. Even with the hot temperature, heat rose from the carcass in waves, bringing a putrid stench with it. The scene didn't look like your typical hunt. Besides being shot, the deer's throat and stomach had been slashed open, and an antler had been sawed off. I gagged.

My father hunted, but when he killed a deer, he didn't toss the body aside and take only parts. He'd prepare the meat and help Mama cook meals from it. This had to be the work of a poacher. Dierk Robinson! He wasn't on the lake with Papa, and maybe he was taking out deer for fun the way he'd slaughtered the rhino.

A motor droned in the distance, and I caught a glimpse of an older truck, though it was too far away to see what color it was. I couldn't be sure where the truck was heading. Normally, my camouflage colors weren't a problem, but if I'd worn something brighter, it would've been harder for Dierk or whoever was out here to mistake me for an animal.

What was I supposed to do? Stay put and stand tall, or run for my life out of the woods? It might not have been the right move, but I crouched down behind the brush. The overgrowth hid me, but it also masked my view.

Not being able to see nearly made me hyperventilate. The hunter might've had me in his sight at this exact moment.

Bigfoot tearing me apart limb by limb had to be the one of the worst ways to die. Getting mistakenly blasted with a shotgun had to be a close second. If Dierk made the mistake of shooting me, he'd never tell anyone. Would he bury me out here? Maybe the team would find my bike off of Old 134, and they'd wonder the rest of their lives what happened to me. My eyes burned, but I couldn't give in to the urge to cry. Not when it would only draw more attention to me than my irregular breathing already had.

I tried to come up with my own Chuck Norris fact. It didn't come to me right away, but here it is: death doesn't flash before your eyes. That was just Chuck Norris doing a roundhouse kick.

BANG!

I jumped and expected to feel sharp pain.

The gun blasted again before I realized that the truck had turned around. The poacher must've moved on to kill something else, probably at the location of another deer blind or trap. I exhaled until I became paranoid that maybe the hunter had shot at one of the others if they'd come looking for me.

I nearly lost my popover from earlier. Once the wave of nausea passed, I crept out of my hiding place, ready to help my brother or Tim or Shawna if something had happened to them. As exposed as could be, I headed into the clearing to find my way back.

I'd observed my surroundings earlier, but where was the path? The charred tree? It might've been for the best to avoid the poacher's route had it not meant I was lost.

18

I'd originally walked to the east to enter the woods, and I'd have to walk back to the west. Like a fool, I'd forgotten the new compass at home.

The sun was so high it didn't provide any clues. I listened for any other gun blasts. The woods were oddly silent.

I'm not sure if I've ever prayed so much all at once. I said a prayer of thanks that I hadn't been killed ... yet. I also prayed I'd make it out of there alive and that Emmett, Tim, and Shawna were all okay.

I walked a ways before another whistle sounded, this one lighter in tone. I almost dropped to the ground, but like I'd been compelled to follow it before, I followed it now. A twig snapped. Then leaves rustled. I couldn't see anything, but I let the whistles guide me.

My adrenaline pumped as I hiked, keeping me from noticing I'd been climbing a hill until I reached a lookout. I could see Old 134!

While the location of my bike wasn't obvious from the lookout, freedom was near. Dierk probably wouldn't dare shoot something this close to the road to risk being discovered, would he? I wasn't going to stick around long enough to find out.

I raced downhill.

I could've kissed the gravel when I reached the road even though I still had to find my bike. I peered over my shoulder in case someone or something was coming after me, but the only person on the road right now was me, and I walked an entire layer of the sole of my sneakers off before I found Gramps' bike.

While it had been a struggle to bike earlier, the remaining nerves helped me push through the difficulties. In fact, my legs pedaled numbly. I glanced to the side of the road looking for pools of blood or something worse than the mutilated deer. I tried to push all the thoughts about what might've happened to my brother or my friends out of my head before I crashed the bike or got sick.

Common sense told me to head to Shawna's mom's house, and no way would I disobey now. Time seemed warped as I biked the remaining distance to the house. And when I got there, I saw the best sight I could've imagined resting against the garage—one girl's and two boys' bikes.

My tank top suctioned to my skin like a damp rag, and my hand wobbled as I rang the doorbell. Ms. Minnoe swung the door open in a dramatic gesture. "Everdil! There you are! Come in, dear." My sweatiness didn't stop her from wrapping her thick arms around me and guiding me inside.

"Where have you been?" Emmett said in a deep voice that reminded me of Papa's when he got mad at us. He sat on the couch near Shawna sipping a glass of lemonade, completely clueless about what I'd just been through.

He had no right to yell at ME! "You broke rule #3—no one gets left behind!" I yelled. I was about to sound off on everyone, but I'm glad I didn't. Shawna's grandmother was stretched out in a hospital-like bed in the center of the room, close to a window. Deep blue and black bruises covered her arm, and she cuddled the stuffed fish I'd given Shawna years ago, Minnoe the Minnow. Unbelievable. She still had it.

These sights put my emotions in check. Somewhat.

"We'll talk about it later," I said to Emmett in a much lower voice. Not sure what else to do, I waved at Shawna's grandmother.

"Hi," she said haltingly. Her smile was friendly even if her right eyelid and lip drooped.

I walked over to her side, careful not to hurt her any more than she'd already been injured from the fall and whatever else she'd been through. "I hope you get better," I told her. I fought tears seeing her like this, plus the magnitude of the ordeal in the woods collapsed in on me.

"You look like you might be thirsty, Everdil," Ms. Minnoe said. "Let me get you a drink. Make yourself comfortable."

No way did I want to sweat on the antique-looking furniture that had been pushed to the side of the room to make way for the bed. My nerves were fired up like a torch about to blast the top of a crème brûlée.

"Grandma liked the popovers," Shawna said in a loud voice, and then when her mom's back turned to us, she whispered, "We were thinking of calling the cops if you didn't show up soon."

"We need to call the cops anyway," I said in a louder voice than I'd intended.

Ms. Minnoe handed me a glass of lemonade. "What was that, Everdil?"

She had enough concerns, so I told another lie after I chugged the lemonade in two gulps. "There was a sheriff who created a roadblock on the highway. That's what took me so long, but everything is okay." The lie came out easy, but it was a stretch since not much criminal activity happened out in these parts, though people like Swamp Sam obviously had gotten in trouble in the past.

"Huh," Ms. Minnoe said, and as she started to say something else, Shawna's grandmother moaned. "Sorry. If you'll excuse me, I need to get Mom's medicine," she said, heading back to the kitchen after grabbing our empty glasses.

Shawna stood up from the floral couch. "We should go now," she said, and the boys followed her lead. "I'll be coming home soon."

Ms. Minnoe exhaled loudly when we said goodbye, which kind of reminded me of my mom. "Thanks for stopping by and for the treats. Please visit as often as you can. I've missed seeing all of your faces, especially yours, Shawna. We're anxious for you to come home." She hugged Shawna so tight that the air whomped out of her.

Even if things weren't perfect with Shawna's family, you could tell how much her mom cared about her. Shawna lingered for a moment.

Emmett pushed me outside with Tim in tow. "You can't just take off like that. What were you thinking? You could get both of us in some serious trouble," he said, getting all Papa-ish on me again.

"You *ditched* me! I heard something strange enough that I needed to check it out." I hesitated for a moment to share what I'd come across, and while I'd been mostly holding it together, I sort of lost it—tears, hiccups, and all. Tim patted me on the back, and I stepped to the side worrying about how gross I was and how much I probably stunk. Shawna came outside right then, and I shared the rest of what happened.

"Did you see the shooter, Everdil?" Emmett asked.

"No, but something supernatural seemed to be happening," I said and explained the whistles. "I have a feeling the poacher has a missing finger." I added how Papa suspiciously had the day off.

"Dierk Robinson," Shawna and Tim said at the same time.

Even though Shawna had to know I officially liked Tim, she play-punched his arm. "Jinx."

Tim ignored her. "This is serious—we need to let my dad know. Do you think you're okay to bike to the park so we can talk to him, Everdil?"

My body was a strange combo of amped up and exhausted. More than anything, I wanted the authorities to catch Dierk before he involved my dad any more than he already had. I held my fist out. "We should still explore the park. I have a feeling we're getting close."

Tim connected his knuckles with mine. "Team Bigfoot," he said. All four of us bumped fists and set off to Caddo Lake State Park.

19

After a few miles, we passed Fyffe's Corner Grocery before turning onto the main park road. The park headquarters was so old it must've been built before Gramps was born.

When we stepped into the main building, a woman named Bessie smiled and greeted us. "Well, look who's here—it's the Nash boy, the Jackson kids, and the pretty girl! Shannon, right?"

"Shawna, actually," Shawna said and smiled at her.

Ouch. There were far more important things to worry about than Bessie's rude comment, but in that moment, all I could think about was how I'd never be considered the pretty one in Shawna's shadow. Not to mention the fact she was a teenager, and I was a lowly twelve-year-old, an age that had no category other than "child" or "pre-teen."

"Is my dad here?" Tim asked.

"He's in his office."

"Thanks."

We followed Tim as he led us to a small office with the door wide open. The room was empty, so while we waited for Mr. Nash to return, Tim showed us a few things. He unlocked a cabinet in the back of the office that was cluttered with a bunch of papers, including an article that Mr. Nash had written called "Bigfoot: Primate's Biological Cousin?" There was a picture of a young Mr. Nash with much thinner glasses standing with an arm around Tim's mom. She cradled a baby Tim dressed up in a monkey costume. Mr. Nash was smiling, and you could see he was bananas over his baby boy and how he dwarfed him in size.

"Check this out," Tim said, pulling out a fragment of a large, yellowed bone. "Dad found this a week ago. He thinks it might be a section of a femur from a dead Bigfoot. An expert's going to check it out."

"Dead Bigfoot, sounds like a band name," Emmett said.

"Be careful with that!" Mr. Nash said as he walked into his office with a mug of steaming coffee in his hand. Tim nearly dropped the piece of femur or whatever it happened to be.

"Sorry," Tim said. "I only wanted to show the team a Bigfoot bone."

Mr. Nash set his coffee on a coaster that had a caricature of Bigfoot with the words "Caddo Critter" below the drawing. "Team?"

"Team. Gang. Friends. Whatever. That's not why we're here—Everdil witnessed something, Dad," Tim said. He had beads of sweat above his lip that looked like a watery mustache.

Mr. Nash turned to me, and I told him what had happened, but he interrupted me and pulled a small recorder out of his pocket. "Everdil, would you mind if I recorded your report? I'll use it as part of the investigation and perhaps at the next Bigfoot conference."

"That's fine." I sounded like a chicken when I explained how I hid behind the brush and didn't manage to get a description of the poacher. I wanted to leave out the part about feeling sick and running away, but I mentioned it to be as accurate for the investigation as possible. "I think the poacher might've been Dierk Robinson," I blurted out and shared why.

Mr. Nash clicked the recorder off. "He's armed and has a deadly intent when it comes to Bigfoot. That much is clear, but I don't get why he'd mutilate a deer. I'll look into this. While I understand and can appreciate your interest in the contest and finding Bigfoot, you all need to be extremely careful."

"Yes, sir," the four of us answered as if we were repeating after a teacher.

We kept his advice in mind as we collected our bikes to investigate the park. Had it not been a safe, poacher-free place, I might've been too freaked to explore.

We pedaled along the main park road to where a few older ladies with binoculars gathered at the end of the observation pier on Sawmill Pond. We ditched our bikes and joined them down the wooden walkway. They weren't witnessing an upright ape walking, like the lady in the local newspaper article, just a pair of wood ducks, a light brown female and a colorful male. When I took a picture of the ducks, the female made a squealing noise that sounded like *ooo-eek*. In the distance, jet skis rumbled.

It was clear we weren't going to find any Bigfoot clues around here. We walked back to our bikes, and I brought up the article. "Where exactly did that lady spot Bigfoot?"

"Good question," Shawna said which made me feel like we were actually on a team together.

"Up a rugged footpath over this way," Tim said, leading us near some hiking trails.

The four of us started out on the trail together, but my energy deflated like a soufflé taken out of the oven too soon. I saw that happen once on an episode of Garbage Can Gourmet.

"C'mon, Everdil Pickle Breath," Emmett said. "Hit me up with some ingredients."

"Please don't call me that." I stopped to rest for a moment. "Carrots, stale popcorn … I can't think of anything else," I said.

Shawna stopped walking. "How about marshmallows?"

"And nightcrawlers," Tim added, his voice squeaking again.

"No," Emmett said. "You have to use edible ingredients."

"Nightcrawlers are edible. Ask any fish." Tim's voice cracked before it went back to normal.

"Okay, if I had to use those gigantic worms, I'd blend them

with the other ingredients together to make a carrot cake."

"My brother makes a mean cream cheese frosting," I said. "You guys go on ahead. I'll stay right here."

"I'm not leaving you," Emmett said. I wanted Tim to be the one to say that, but it was nice not to be left alone even if it was with my brother.

Shawna and Tim took off together. She kept looking up at him as she jabbered on about something. I wanted to know what they were talking about, but then again, maybe I didn't.

"You shouldn't have gone off in the woods by yourself, Everdil," Emmett scolded.

"We've already established that. You would've done the same thing if you'd heard the noises that I had. Besides, I thought you'd come after me."

Emmett lowered his voice. "I should've. Please don't tell Mama and Papa."

I'd leave my parents out of this because I would've gotten in more trouble than Emmett, but I hesitated like I was really thinking it over. "You'll have to bake me something special," I said. Don't judge. You'd resort to culinary blackmail too considering the tasty things my brother makes, minus that red velvet cake, of course.

"Guys!" Shawna called out, loud enough that she could've scared away those ducks on the pond. "I found something!"

The path was steep, but that didn't slow me or Emmett down.

"I found footprints," Shawna said when we reached her.

She had found prints alright, and while they sort of looked like the casts we'd seen, these were smaller, sort of like Emmett's height compared to Tim's. I took a few pictures of the prints.

Tim moved his foot next to the footprints for comparison. His boots were unlaced. He had pretty big feet for his age, and the prints were only slightly bigger than the size of his shoe. "Something else probably made these."

"It could be Littlefoot," Emmett joked.

"You're funny," Shawna responded.

"Funny looking," I said under my breath.

As we continued hiking, I discovered a monster-sized pile of poop near the rocks not too far away from the footprints. "Think Bigfoot had an emergency?"

"Or an enormous dog dropped a deuce," Emmett said.

After Tim inspected the pile, he said, "Based on the contents, it looks more like bear scat than a dog's diet, but Louisiana black bears no longer live in this area."

"Maybe some decided to vacation in Texas," Shawna said.

"Ha ha," Emmett said.

While it was doubtful Bigfoot had gone potty here, it was just as doubtful that the world's largest dog had either. Not to be gross, but the poop didn't look like dog poop, either—small white bones and balls of grass were mixed in with the grossness. For the sake of documenting our mission, I bent down slightly to get a zoomed in photo of the pile.

When I aimed the camera, Emmett pretended like he was going to push me into the pile. Even though he barely touched me, I lost my balance and fell backwards. I managed to correct myself ... only too much. My knee ended up landing in the icky mess.

You would've thought this was the most comical thing that ever happened in our whole time together based on the team's laughter.

I'd never wanted a bath so badly in my whole entire life and wanted to get away from there and away from my *teammates*.

Emmett held his hand out to help me up, but I pushed it away. "I was only messing around," he said. Like that was a real apology.

I wanted to think of a comeback so good it would've made him feel more rotten and disgusting than what coated my knee, but the urge to start crying hit me again. This day had gone from bad to worse, and other than the filthy stain, I had nothing to show for it.

Without saying a word, I took off down the trail.

"Wait up," Tim said.

No way was I going to wait up for him or for the others. I had nothing to say to those stooges the entire way home, but I will say this—we at least stuck together. Emmett brought up the Ingredient Game, but it fizzled out without me participating, and I had to admit, it improved my mood a little to know they couldn't do something without me.

20

Emmett made chocolate mousse with homemade whipped cream for dinner while Mama and Papa were at work, but considering what it looked like, well, it sort of seemed like another jab at me. Plus, he gave Shawna the largest portion even though he was trying to make up with me, not her.

Tim devoured the mousse Emmett had saved for him while we waited for Gramps to pick us up for the boat tour the next day. Then he raided our fridge and helped himself to some macaroni and cheese that he ate cold, straight from the dish. Tim talked with his mouth full just like his dad. "Dierk Robinson said he had an explanation for his whereabouts yesterday morning, though he can't prove it with a witness. The game warden's on his case."

"He seems guilty to me," Shawna said. She washed the dishes

like she was right at home, too. The break was nice.

"Dierk could've just been shopping around for a new finger," Emmett said which was a lame joke. He stood up a few moments later when Gramps pulled in the driveway. "Shotgun!" He raced outside, and the rest of us followed.

"I've got one heck of a tour planned," Gramps said as he opened the large door of his not-so-large VW Bug for us. "Let's get this party started!"

"I don't mind sitting in the middle," I offered as the three of us debated spots after Emmett had claimed the best one.

"That's okay. I'll do it," Shawna said, getting in the car first to take the middle spot. Maybe she thought she was doing me a favor, but she had to know I wanted to sit next to Tim. Was she into him too? That could've explained her reaction after I told her I thought he liked her. My insides felt squashed in more ways than one when she stuffed herself next to me.

"So how is the hunt going?" Gramps asked, looking at us in the rearview mirror when he really should've been keeping his eyes on the road. He turned a corner a little too fast.

"Did the boys tell you …" I started to ask, but Shawna squeezed the words right out of me when she mashed into me after Gramps clipped a curb.

"I figured it out, and even if I hadn't, your outfits are a dead giveaway. I've been doing some hunting myself lately. Got your camera, Everdil?"

I held it up and prayed for as much luck as possible.

Gramps took us out on a different part of the lake than the usual boat path, past Alligator Bayou. The water had the same consistency as homemade pea soup, and the sky appeared gooey with dense, dark clouds. We didn't see any alligators, but there sure were a lot of cypress trees growing along the banks. Some of the gnarled trees had to be hundreds of years old, and the roots jutting out of the swamp seemed like creepy gnomes watching us as we passed on by. A musty odor clung to the air.

"Hey Gramps, what do you know about Dierk Robinson?" Emmett asked.

"I can't say, but I've been keeping track of where Dierk and your dad have been heading. In fact, I'm taking you to one of the most recent places they visited." Gramps turned around and winked at us. The boat swerved a bit. Shawna grabbed the boat rail just like I did. My grandfather isn't the best driver, but even then, he's far more skilled than me.

We soon passed Alligator Island, which was covered in pine trees. So many of these places around the lake looked as if nobody had ever stepped foot on them. You can't access much of Caddo Lake without a boat—no wonder Bigfoot would choose to live around here given the excess of land, water, and food sources. I imagined Bigfoot could swim by using those giant arms as paddles. I kept my camera at the ready in case he made an appearance.

"This place looks haunted," Shawna said.

At that mention, Emmett scooted a little closer to her and

Gramps went into storytelling mode.

"Harrison County is supposedly the most haunted county in all of Texas. Some people believe that Old Stagecoach Road in Marshall happens to be the most haunted place in all of the world."

Just hearing the word "haunted" repeated several times gave me the chills, especially since the clouds began to drizzle. I waited to see if Tim inched his way on the bench closer to me, though if he moved at all, it was just my imagination.

"I've never seen anything with my own two eyes, but I've heard many reports of a ghostly stagecoach and phantom pallbearers lugging around a coffin on Old Stagecoach Road. Other people have said they've seen strange creatures in the area. Legend has it that an apelike boy used to perch himself in the tree canopy and frighten passengers by kicking the top of their stagecoaches."

"Hoo Hoo Wah," a voice called. Emmett jumped up from the bench seat so high it was like he'd gotten shot in the bottom again.

"Hoo Hoo Hoooo Wah."

Gramps chuckled. "Don't worry, Emmett. The apelike boy isn't going to get you—that's just an owl who seems confused."

In all fairness to the owl, it looked much later than it was considering the sky had gotten awfully dark with the rainclouds rolling in.

"I'm not scared," Emmett said, convincing no one. "Did you know ghosts tell Chuck Norris stories?"

"Gram would've liked that fact," Gramps said.

We chatted about how the creatures and the boy could've been related to Bigfoot as Gramps guided the boat close to the banks of Goat Island. It was slow going to navigate through the patches of giant salvinia. The plants choked up the engine just as much as it was suffocating the plants and fish in this part of the lake.

Before we stepped off the boat, I grabbed a flashlight and checked to make sure the camera was tucked in the bag so it wouldn't get wet in case it started to do more than sprinkle. Goat Island had never looked so creepy. The moss hanging from the cypress trees appeared like giant webs, and I could almost imagine monster-sized spiders dangling from the branches.

As we made our way down an overgrown footpath, a twig moved amongst the dead leaves right near Emmett. Flashing the light, I could see it wasn't a twig. Dad had taught me how to recognize the bands and the reddish brown-gold color since we spent so much time at the lake. "Copperhead!" I yelled.

Emmett cried out before lunging forward. The snake un-coiled, striking at his ankle.

"It got me!" Emmett stumbled, but kept on running.

"You need to calm down, or you'll make things worse," Tim

called after him.

A sinking feeling overwhelmed me as we rushed over to Emmett. Copperheads are poisonous. Deadly poisonous.

Emmett was hunched over, pressing a hand against his stomach.

"Are you okay?" Shawna asked.

Emmett was ashen and sweaty. His breathing slowed. Then it became more labored.

"Of course he's not okay!" I yelled. There was a good chance Emmett might not survive the bite. My insides felt as though they were filling with the poisonous toxin, too.

Gramps pulled out a pocketknife and was ready to dig out the poison with the blade before Tim stopped him. "That will make it worse," Tim said.

I would've been willing to suck out the poison or do whatever to save my brother's life, but I knew from those TV rescue shows that the best thing to do was keep Emmett calm and take him to a hospital.

Shawna cried.

"It's going to be okay," Tim told her.

What a complete lie, but it had to be okay. I couldn't lose my brother. "Malted milk powder, canned beans, onion rings, and corn flakes. Think fast, Emmett!"

Emmett ignored my Ingredient Game. He lifted his pants leg up. His sock was tinged with blood near the ankle.

"Well, I'll be," Gramps said as he took a closer look.

"What's wrong?" I asked. Yelled is more like it.

"Doesn't look like a snake bite to me," Gramps said.

"Are you sure? It burns and my heart's pounding harder than it ever has before." Emmett bent down to inspect his ankle.

"I think your grandpa's right," Tim said. "There aren't any fang marks."

Emmett groaned. The fang marks weren't obvious if they were there at all. Above the bloody part of his sock was what looked like a deep scratch dotted with a line of blood.

"We should get you to a hospital, just in case," I said. Shawna agreed.

"I think a sharp twig got me when I took off, not the snake," Emmett said, washing his ankle with a bottle of water. "I feel dumb, but I'm fine."

"This was one of Gram's favorites," Gramps started. "Chuck Norris once got bitten by a poisonous snake. After days of pain and agony, the snake died."

Emmett managed to smile.

We should've taken the near snake bite as our cue to leave Goat Island, but we pressed on after taking a moment to catch our breaths.

21

The drizzle had turned into a light rain shower.

"Oh no! My hair's going to get frizzy like yours, Everdil. Should we go home?" Shawna asked.

"Your hair looks great," Tim said. "No reason to head back."

Great.

I ran my fingers through my hair. It had to be a curly disaster.

"There's something I want to show you," Gramps said. He took the lead, and we followed him down a narrow path with weeds so overgrown we were forced to walk single file. I trailed Gramps, followed by Tim, Shawna, and then Emmett. We were extra vigilant for snakes, though Emmett took this to an extreme. I know he'd just experienced a close call, but if he'd been going any slower, he would've gone backwards.

Shawna stayed close to Emmett. I overheard him say something to her like, "I can't believe you cried over me."

"Whatever. Is my makeup getting smudged? Between that and my hair, I think I'm going to die."

"Cause of death? Cosmetic failure," Emmett said.

I heard Shawna laugh.

Gramps led us to a deep hole about six feet deep and wider than his entire arm span. My head swirled as I stared into the pit, especially considering it seemed like a grave of sorts.

Using a flashlight, Gramps spotlighted a thick loblolly pine about ten feet away that had somehow been folded over. "I overheard Dierk Robinson say that he believes Bigfoot is responsible for both of these things."

Other people camped on the island from time to time, but it didn't look like a single soul could've folded a tree like that. Even skeptics might've considered Bigfoot had twisted the pine's trunk—there wasn't a shred of evidence that a saw or any other man-made tool had marked the tree.

Protecting the camera lens from the rain, I photographed the sights, marveling that whatever had bent the pine could surely snap all of us like a twig. The low battery light on my camera started flashing. Ugh! I hadn't charged the battery.

"This is exactly like what we saw near Swamp Sam's place. Right, Emmett?" Tim asked, turning around.

Emmett wasn't there, and neither was Shawna.

"Maybe the apelike boy got 'em!" Gramps started to laugh.

"Please don't say that, Gramps." Like with the snake, my mind went to the worst case scenario—that Bigfoot or a poacher had snatched them. I knew it was unlikely, but so much had happened recently. The island seemed even creepier as thunder boomed way off in the distance. The same musty odor still hung in the air, almost foul, as if a skunk had sprayed nearby.

Maybe my brother and Shawna were pranking us. I doubted it, though. And from Tim's expression, he seemed as worried as me.

"C'mon, guys! We promised we were going to stick together," I called out, which was pointless.

The seriousness of the situation must've sunk in for Gramps because he pulled out his knife again. "They couldn't have gone far," he said.

Tim found a small branch that he carried like a baseball bat as we searched for our lost teammates. I made sure my camera was tucked away safely and picked up my own stick.

The island wasn't that large, and it didn't make sense to me how we could've lost them. While it was doubtful Shawna and Emmett had been kidnapped, there was a chance they might've fallen into a pit like the one Gramps showed us.

"Emmett! Shawna!" we hollered as we continued walking the trail. The air smelled less skunk-like as the wind whipped around.

"We should split up," Tim suggested right as a bolt of lightning streaked overhead. Thunder boomed within six counts of Mississippi.

"I don't like the sounds of that," Gramps said.

I reminded Tim of Rule #3. The rain picked up at that moment, some of the drops zooming down with enough force that they snapped my skin.

"It'll be quicker this way. I'll head to the south," Tim said.

"I still don't like the idea of separating, but the storm is going to hit hard," Gramps said. "Let's yell or whistle to each other in case something happens." He whistled three times for practice, which I'm sure he thought was reassuring, but the shrill sound made my toxic stomach feeling return.

As I set off on a trail near the water to the east, alone and drenched, more lightning flashed in the sky. The brightness reflecting off of the lake created an eerie effect.

Something scuttled near the knobby knees of the cypress trees. "Emmett? Shawna?" I couldn't see any details other than a black shadow that dipped under a blanket of spatterdock. This obviously wasn't Emmett or Shawna. From the way a row of the plants moved, the creature was trying to get away. Whatever it was, it looked to be about alligator-sized though longer and wider.

Bigfoot was most definitely a possibility. Perhaps that could explain the musky, skunky smell. It was pointless to take a picture in this lighting when the battery was nearly dead and the storm could destroy the camera.

As I turned around, lightning lit up the sky and helped me to see where I was going despite the sheets of rain. I managed to spot a group of several large red-eared sliders huddled on the banks not too far from where I saw the shadow creature. One turtle dug the mushy ground as if it were about to bury some eggs, and it made me wonder if that's what the shadow creature had been hunting for.

The rain made it difficult to see where I was going, and the trail was a muddy mess with pools of water collecting. "Emmett! Shawna!" I called out again as I ventured north.

I stopped when I heard one shrill whistle followed by another. And then another. The whistles came from the west and sounded exactly like Gramps' practice ones. Either he had gotten lost or something awful had happened.

My clothes and entire body were weighed down from the rain and from worrying as I bolted in the direction of the sound. I made the mistake of not looking up from the ground as I headed what I thought was west, and when I did, a shadowy figure charged right at me.

I screamed before being tackled to the ground, but not before I took a swing at whatever was coming at me.

22

I had a vision that I was at a water park and Tim was smiling at me as he helped me up from a squishy inner-tube.

He moved in close, and his face was only inches from mine. His eyes almost looked cross-eyed as I stared at him. My heart was on a roller coaster ride of its own—was he going to try to kiss me?

I held my breath in anticipation.

But a surge of pain zapped me instead. I tried to yell, but Tim had one hand on my jaw.

"Please don't move," he said. "Your mouth is bleeding, and I'm making sure you're okay."

My brain slowly caught up to reality. I wasn't at a water park. I was on Goat Island in the middle of a bad storm, and I'd gotten attacked. The squishy inner-tube was nothing but a stretch of mud that I'd collapsed on. And Tim said my mouth was bleeding.

I nearly passed out again.

"Nothing looks broken, but there's blood coming from the gum area around your front tooth," Tim said.

My tongue reached for the spot, and I sensed the rawness of the tissue and tasted blood. My front tooth, the one that didn't overlap, wiggled loosely.

I tried to regulate my breathing by thinking calm thoughts. My mind returned to the water park vision. My mouth throbbed.

"What's going on?" an approaching voice asked.

I didn't dare turn my head, but I could just barely see Emmett out of the corner of my eye—he looked like he was coated in blood. I stopped breathing altogether.

It wasn't until he got closer that I realized it wasn't blood, just reddish-brown dirt stains. Shawna was with him and Gramps too. They were all very much alive and just as filthy.

"Everything okay?" Emmett asked, his voice softer now.

"Everdil hurt her mouth. It was an accident. I heard the whistles and ran to help, but I thought I saw something and … I, I ran into your sister." Tim's hand shook.

"You did what to her?" Emmett asked.

I squirmed. "He said it was an accident. We collided."

I couldn't believe Tim had been the one who had ambushed me. I also couldn't believe my front tooth was loose. Would it fall out?

Tim let go of my mouth, but kept his other hand on my jaw for a moment. "I'm really sorry, Everdil."

At this, I cried, not that it was obvious in the rain. I was twelve, and the thought of looking like a toothless six-year-old was too much for me to take on top of everything else. I never thought I'd miss my own snaggletooth.

"You'll be fine, Everdil Pickle," Gramps said. He squeezed me in the most comforting of hugs, his flannel shirt drenched.

Tim exhaled, sounding like a tire with a leak in it.

"We should leave," I said so slowly and carefully. I fought the urge to wiggle the tooth with my finger or my tongue.

Tim ignored me and ground his feet into the mud as he turned towards Shawna and Emmett. "Where did you guys go? We were supposed to stick together!"

I'd never heard him so upset.

"I saw a baby Bigfoot," Shawna blurted out. "Emmett and I tried to track it down, but we got turned around until we found Gramps."

I snorted. "Really? You saw something in this weather? A baby Bigfoot of all things?"

Shawna crossed her arms over her wet clothes that clung to her curves. "Just because you're not the center of attention since you didn't see it for yourself doesn't mean *I* didn't see it."

"Center of attention? That describes *you* not *me*."

"What's that supposed to mean, Ever*dil*?" She drew out my name like an insult.

"You're the one who dresses like she wants everyone to notice her and it's ... it's the way you act, too. Like if I knew my good friend was interested in a boy, I would leave him alone out of respect for her." After saying that aloud, I needed to have my head evaluated and not just my mouth. Good thing I didn't see the boys' reactions or even Gramps' for that matter. I felt so mortified that I wanted to be buried in that deep pit.

"No wonder why I stopped being your friend!" Shawna said.

There. She said it, confirming what I'd been thinking all along.

This hurt far worse than Tim taking me down. "Well, good thing you can quit pretending now."

"Girls, let's not—" Gramps began, but I wasn't willing to hear any of it.

"I want to go home." I took off, not having a sense of direction. A bolt of lightning zipped through the sky, and thunder boomed so loud it rumbled my organs. The storm matched my mood exactly.

We found our way to the boat, but the weather was too tumultuous to return for the time being. We took shelter under the roof of the pontoon, and I sat as far away from everyone as I could.

"I should've been more careful," Tim said, his voice squeaking again.

While we waited the storm out, Gramps spun a story about some storm he and Gram got stuck in, but I couldn't concentrate. *Baby Bigfoot. Center of attention. Stopped being your friend.* These were the things that cycled through my mind besides the pain of taking such a nasty spill. Tim really should've been more careful. *Timmy.* Ugh.

What was supposed to be an exciting adventure had turned

into a nightmare. I refused to be part of the team anymore, not that we were much of a solid team anyway. The whole thing seemed like childish, wishful thinking.

Emmett got up from his cozy spot next to Shawna to talk to me. I scooted away from him, but he placed his arm around my shoulder. I thought he was going to force me to stay put, but his grasp was gentle. You could almost call it a hug. "Sorry," he said which was one of the few times he'd apologized to me. "I got caught up in the excitement."

"Shawna's a liar and a *thief*," I said, loud enough that Shawna turned from talking to Tim to glare at me. If looks could kill, lightning would've touched down from the sky directly on the top of my skull and fried me alive. Who cared about betraying Shawna's confidence? We weren't friends anymore, anyway.

"There's a possibility she's telling the truth. Think about the ape-like boy and those smaller prints we saw at the park near the poop—"

My mind flashed back to the shadowy creature I watched swim off along the banks, too. A younger, smaller Bigfoot capable of swimming might've explained the mystery, but highly unlikely. I didn't want to encourage Shawna or the boys for that matter.

"Leave me alone, Emmett," I told him. "I quit."

"You don't want to quit. You're just upset right now. I would be, too."

"*Please* leave me alone."

"Fine," he said, taking a deep breath that sounded full of

defeat. Before he walked away, he added, "Baked bean casserole."

"Huh?"

"That's what I would've made with those ingredients you gave me earlier. Malted milk powder, canned beans, onion rings, and corn flakes. Thanks for helping me." Without another word, Emmett backed off and resumed his spot close to Shawna and Tim again.

I'd sent him away, I know, but that traitor. The three of them whispered together.

We departed Goat Island when the storm moved on. The boat seemed to slosh around inside and out as we made our way back to Uncertain. Uncertain. That's exactly how I felt.

23

I never quite understood the phrase "flipped on a dime," but it described the moment perfectly when Papa rushed at us, his arms flailing as he cheered, "We did it! We did it!"

Did what, I wondered, but Emmett was quicker to figure things out. (I blame my injury.) "You found Bigfoot?" he hollered as Gramps roped the pontoon to the dock. Emmett jumped off the boat without waiting for it to be properly secured, hitting the ground with a loud thump. He rolled forward.

"Are you okay?" I called out, forgetting for a moment that I was mad at him.

Papa was too crazed to lecture about boat safety. "Dierk and I found a body that most certainly belongs to Bigfoot! Tim, your father's checking things out now along with some other experts.

Where have you all been?" The excitement in his face drained when he got a better look at us.

The steps were so slick that I slipped, but Papa reached for my arm and helped get me off the boat. "You okay, Everdil?" he asked, checking me over just like Mama would've had she not been at work.

My nearly knocked out front tooth must've been obvious. But Papa wasn't inspecting my mouth—he scrutinized patches of blood on my shirt which seemed worse because of the way the rain had spread the stains.

"I take full responsibility, sir," Tim said, stretching out his right shoulder and then rubbing it.

Shawna huffed.

Papa glanced from Tim to Shawna to Gramps for some kind of explanation, but what happened on Goat Island wasn't nearly as important as his news. "Everything's fine," I said, trying to talk as normally as possible. "Just a few bumps, that's all. You found a body?"

Papa's excitement returned, and he talked so fast that it was hard to keep up with him. "I took Dierk to Potter's Point, and we followed some tracks and found an even deeper pit than before. This one was covered in cypress branches, and once we moved them out of the way, I discovered an enormous ape-like body lying on the bottom. At first, I thought the creature was sleeping, but Dierk—," Papa said, hesitating before he said, "well, it doesn't matter, but I saw a pool of blood. It's the real thing. I know it. We left the body the way we found it and came back immediately to notify the experts."

I believed Papa even though I faced some doubt moments before. Or at least I wanted to believe him because if he was right, the end result would be the same despite how badly Team Bigfoot had failed—winning the contest and snagging the million dollars.

Chatter and questions about what would happen next flew about like debris in a tornado.

"We have to wait, and the storm's caused even more delays. I couldn't go back to the site until I knew you were all okay," Papa said, running his hands along his stubble. "I was getting worried."

He had no idea what we'd been through. When we went inside the marina, Papa got us some towels, but drying off wasn't a priority. The fact that my father found a Bigfoot body and had a claim to a million dollar contest should've seemed more important in that moment, but all I could focus on was my tooth.

I locked myself in the tiny bathroom, cringing when I glanced in the bathroom mirror. The outside of my lip was swollen and the inside was an angry red. Despite the looseness, my front tooth looked normal though the gum line appeared to have been outlined in purple marker.

I wish I could tell you that I prayed over Bigfoot and the money or for forgiveness for the fight I had with Shawna, but instead I prayed, "Dear God, let me keep my tooth."

When I stepped out of the bathroom, Papa approached me with a storm-cloud-like expression. "Tim told me what happened, and Shawna helped me look up an emergency dental clinic in Shreveport that can see you tonight if we can get there before eight. We can make it if we leave right now."

"I'm fine," I lied again. "There are much more important things than a tooth." I looked over at Shawna who was on her cell phone again. "I'm not trying to be the center of attention or anything."

I couldn't tell if Shawna heard this or not, but at least the boys did as they stood nearby listening to our conversation. Emmett paced back in forth as if I was going to rat him out somehow.

"I know you're not faking this, Everdil, and besides, driving you to the clinic will help pass the time until the experts take pictures of the body and can remove it safely from the pit. I'll follow up as soon as we get back."

"It'll be expensive—"

Papa held up his hand to stop me from saying anything more. "The cost shouldn't be a concern, and maybe we won't have to worry about finances for a while," Papa said, smiling. Sure, he got things stuck in his teeth frequently, but I never realized just how nice his teeth were. Funny how something like an accident makes you appreciate things like this. "It might make the difference between you being able to save your tooth or not," he added.

Okay, that got to me.

"I accept financial responsibility, Mr. Jackson. I'll pay you back by working my debt off at the marina."

"Thank you, Tim, but that won't be necessary."

"I'll make it up to Everdil if she'll let me," Tim said, like I wasn't standing right in front of him. He studied me for a reaction.

I didn't give him the satisfaction of one. I even refused to say goodbye to anyone but Gramps as we separated.

"Chin up, Everdil Pickle," Gramps said. "When Chuck Norris kicks things apart, they fall back together in place." He kissed me on the cheek.

I wasn't sure if Gramps was going to drive the rest of the "team" home or if they'd attempt to get in on the Bigfoot action. *I don't care,* I thought. I couldn't even convince myself.

The Louisiana border wasn't too far away from Uncertain, but the drive to Shreveport, one of the larger cities around, took over an hour. Even with the excitement of the discovery, Papa's rumbly truck lulled me into a deep sleep.

Papa nudged me awake as I dreamed about turtles backstroking alongside bear-like creatures in Caddo Lake. He parked in front of a brightly lit dentist office that stood out on the otherwise dark street.

My hands slicked with sweat as we made our way inside—this was much worse than getting my teeth cleaned and who knows what the dentist would do with my tooth in this kind of state.

A man, woman, and a young boy sat in the waiting room when we walked inside, and they stared at us as if we'd crawled out of the swamp. Considering what a mess we both were and the events that led us here, I suppose it wasn't too far from the truth. I attempted to smile at them, but it must've been more like a grimace because of my swollen lip. The boy frowned and the family turned their stares from us to the TV. The local news repeated on a loop.

I focused on the news rather than the many toothsome diagrams and brochures around the office while Papa filled out paperwork.

"So did Tim run into you before or after you hit him?" Papa asked as he scribbled a few things down.

I'd forgotten about taking a swing before getting knocked out. Tim hadn't said anything about it or even complained. To make things worse, I'd treated him terribly after he was trying to help me. "Is he okay?"

"You got him square in the shoulder, and other than some soreness, I suspect he'll be fine. You've got a good arm on you, Everdil." Papa smiled before getting up to turn the form into the receptionist who said it would be a few more minutes.

Shortly after the other family was called to the back office, the news stopped repeating, and an anchor with more makeup than Shawna came on to announce the "news of the weird."

"This is just in—Dierk Robinson, a representative in Dallas, is reported to have found the body of Sasquatch in Uncertain, Texas." The camera zoomed in on a photo of a large, furry beast scrunched up at the bottom of a muddy, watery pit. "Is this a certain or an uncertain find? We'll have to wait and see," the news anchor said in such a sing-songy way my blood pressure elevated.

It must've had the same effect on Papa. "That son of a gun!" he said.

The news anchor didn't mention Papa or Raleigh's Tours, which wasn't fair considering he was the one actually responsible for finding the body. And he was here with me in Louisiana and couldn't get it straightened out in person.

Instead of the Ingredients Game, a different one pounded my mind where I listed the items I wished had gone differently.

Our "team" would've been the one to find Bigfoot, not Dierk Robinson.

I would've turned Shawna away that day she showed up on my stoop.

Tim wouldn't have busted up my mouth, he would've …

"Everdil Jackson?" a dental assistant called.

Papa and I got up but turned around as we walked to the back office in case the news reported anything else. The only thing on was a fast food commercial featuring a Texas-sized burger. My stomach grumbled.

The dental assistant sat me in one of those awful chairs and asked me to explain what happened. I condensed things majorly. "I was out exploring when one of my friends ran into me and knocked my tooth loose."

The assistant took a quick peek inside my mouth. "Ouch. The dentist should be here in a moment."

While we waited again, Papa tapped his foot and twisted his lips, like he was about to get his mouth worked on as well. I know he wanted to be back home sorting out the truth, not stuck here with me.

"Welcome, but sorry you're here," the dentist said when she entered the room. She was an older woman with a friendly smile though her teeth were unnaturally white. She asked me to repeat the story I'd told the receptionist as she looked at my chart. "Uncertain, Texas, huh? I just heard on 'news of the weird' that a politician found a Bigfoot body there. Were you the one to discover it?" she joked. She snort-laughed and had no idea how close to home her comment hit both me and Papa.

"I wish," I answered.

"What an incredible story that would make," the dentist said. "Now open wide."

She asked the same questions the assistant did, but I don't know how she expected me to answer with my mouth open like that. Papa filled her in.

"There aren't any guarantees, but your tooth is in good condition and will hopefully heal without any lasting complications." The dentist explained how she was putting in a dental splint to hold my tooth in place while it firmly reattached itself. Hopefully.

I wondered how my tooth would look once it healed. Would it overlap just as much if not more? The splint felt foreign against my tongue, but there was comfort in knowing my tooth wouldn't plop out of the socket and choke me in my sleep.

While Papa made arrangements for the bill, which I'm sure was huge, I stood near the TV hoping for and also dreading another Bigfoot update. Papa glanced over at the screen, but all that was on now was the local weather report. The meteorologist predicted a streak of hot temperatures.

"Thanks for taking me," I told Papa on the way home. "Sorry for what happened and that Dierk didn't give you credit."

Papa had to be going at least ten to fifteen miles over the speed limit, but he eased up on the truck's accelerator when he patted my knee. "Not to worry, Everdil. We'll work things out. The marina might start bringing in some money soon, and I can take on another job. I'm a good dishwasher like you."

He put a smile on his face, but it couldn't hide his disappointment. "What's important is that you're okay. We're all okay."

Things weren't okay, though, and once again, I'd ruined everything, just like Emmett had said on my birthday.

24

"Any update?" Papa asked Mama as she rushed out the front door to meet us wearing her sleeping t-shirt and boxers.

"First, fill me in on what's more important," Mama said, inspecting my face.

"Everdil's tooth should be okay," Papa said and then repeated what the dentist had said. "She's quite a trooper."

Mama whisked me inside and presented me with a plate of sliced bananas coated in a chocolate sauce so heavenly that angels would endorse it. Papa grabbed two beers from the fridge, taking a long drink from one of the bottles before he passed the other to Mama.

"Is Emmett home?" I asked between chocolatey mouthfuls.

"He's sleeping," Mama said as she brought me a napkin along

with an ice pack.

While it was late, this didn't seem like Emmett, especially since he had to be curious about everything going on. "What about Shawna?" I asked.

"Her grandmother's had some major improvements, and she went home to spend time with her family," Mama said. "Is everything okay between the two of you?"

"She's not the friend I thought she was."

"Seems to me that Shawna's just trying to find her way. You may not even be aware of it, but you are, too. Twelve is a hard age. You just need to be the friend you've always been, Everdil."

"Sure," I said, and just as I began to tell Mama about the Louisiana Bigfoot news clip to change the subject, the home phone rang.

"You get it, Raleigh," Mama said. "The phone has been ringing off the hook."

This was encouraging. Raleigh's tours must've been mentioned on some type of news source.

"Hello?" Papa asked in his deep voice. There was a long pause as he listened to the caller and then said, "Thanks for the interest, but you'll have to call the marina in the morning to schedule a tour."

After he gave the marina's phone number and hung up, Mama told Papa. "Gramps said the tours are booked completely solid for the next two months."

Papa smiled his toothsome smile. "You're kidding!"

"No jokes here, unlike a few of the other calls." After sipping her beer, she mocked one of them. "Why did someone drop out of the contest to find Bigfoot?"

I shrugged at the same time Papa answered, "I don't know. Why?"

"Because he couldn't face de-feet! Get it? De-feet!"

The joke was so dumb that it made me laugh.

Even Mama did. "At least that call was entertaining unlike some of the other ones. Swamp Sam rang us up to say we should sell the marina immediately and something about an invading army. I wasn't sure if he meant a Bigfoot army or what because he sounded drunk. I offered to bring him dinner or hinted that I'd be happy to drive him to an appointment if he needed, but he hung up on me. And then some environmentalist called to say we should be punished for exposing Bigfoot and shooting such a special being in its sleep."

Shoot Bigfoot in its sleep? So that was the part of the story Papa had left out—how cowardly of Dierk Robinson! It shouldn't have surprised me given what he did to that rhinoceros.

Papa took another sip of his beer. "Sorry you had to deal with those calls, Macy. I can't imagine why Dierk went to the media immediately. I take it back, I can, but it doesn't make sense to me why he didn't hold off a while longer. After I call him, let's disconnect the line."

He looked over at me, and I took this as my cue that he wanted some privacy.

"Goodnight," I said, as I poured myself a glass of tepid water to wash down the film of chocolate stuck to the roof of my mouth. "Thanks for taking good care of me."

I needed to shower and brush my teeth, carefully of course, but first I checked in on Emmett. He'd pulled the covers over his head so all that was visible was the lump of his body. His head looked smaller than normal. When I tiptoed in for a closer inspection, it was just a pile of clothing bunched up in a ball. The lump of his body was nothing more than pillows. That sneak!

I turned around back into the living room and was about to enter the kitchen when I heard Papa yell, "That's unacceptable, Dierk! I'm only asking for a small percentage. What? You signed the contract, too, and you can't get out of paying me for my services—"

Mama got up to rub Papa's shoulders. I ducked back into the hallway to go shower as planned.

While I waited for the water to heat up, I fumed. I couldn't believe Dierk was trying to swindle Papa! My parents needed this money to pay the bills and to settle things with the bank. It was great Papa had so many tours lined up in the upcoming months, but that didn't help matters now.

With this news combined with the other stresses, I held off on reporting Emmett. Maybe he had a good reason for sneaking off, plus Mama and Papa would freak out, making an already bad situation worse.

Emmett was going to owe me big time! He could've been in danger, but I had a gut feeling he was fine, *and* that he wasn't alone. When I walked into my room, all of Shawna's stuff was gone.

The pallet on the floor and the new wall color were the only reminders that she'd been here for a few days. The texture of the wallpaper remnants stood out, bothering me that Shawna had practically vandalized my room. Yes, the wallpaper had been too much, but now my plain bumpy walls seemed too little.

Maybe I would get some posters—stuff *I* wanted like artistic photos of landscapes or animals. Speaking of animals, I rescued my stuffed pigs from the closet, setting a few back on my bed and a couple on my dresser.

I wondered if Shawna had really gone home. Papa was off the phone, and it hadn't been disconnected yet. No luck. Shawna's cell phone went straight to voicemail. I called Tim to see if I could find answers or if he was missing like Emmett, but his dad must've disconnected their home line, too, because I kept getting a busy signal.

Through my closed door, Mama and Papa argued about the money crisis. I thought about sneaking out of the house, but where would I have started to look for them? Potter's Point, where Papa and Dierk had found the pit with the Bigfoot body? That thought was enough to give me a wicked case of the shivers. Potter's Point had been named after Robert Potter, some guy who was murdered who knows how long after signing the Texas Declaration of Independence. He's not buried there anymore, but Papa weaved all kinds of tales of his ghost haunting the area. I closed my eyes and prayed Emmett and the others knew what they were doing, wherever they were.

There are several unpleasant ways to wake up in the morning, like when your brother puts your hand in warm water to see if you'll embarrass yourself or when he thumps you in the head with a pillow. But these things seemed like a minor nuisance compared to the sound of the doorbell ringing and seeing a sheriff's car parked in your driveway.

I should've said something to Mama and Papa about Emmett's disappearance. They were clueless, and what if the sheriff was here to tell us ... I didn't dare finish that thought.

Papa shook the sheriff's hand and let him in. "Thanks for coming," Papa said.

Wait, what? Was Papa the one who called the police?

"Everdil, would you give us a moment?" Papa asked, much clearer this time that he wanted privacy.

"Sure," I said, walking slowly back to my room to see what I could overhear. I heard the word "bullets" and something about illegal weapons. The sheriff had to be here on account of Dierk Robinson.

Mama caught me in the hallway, standing near the closet leaning in to eavesdrop. "Listen to your papa, Everdil. Why don't you shower up, and I can make you something for breakfast before I go to work. It'll help calm my nerves," she added.

I'd already showered last night, but my hair looked like a curly heron's nest after sleeping on it while my hair was damp. I pulled my hair back into a ponytail, and as soon as Mama headed into the kitchen, I checked on Emmett.

I hoped to see his real body there, not the lump of the pillow still. The clothing ball was slightly exposed.

I was torn. There was a sheriff sitting in my living room talking to my father. Should I tell on Emmett now that he hadn't come home yet? Or would this cause my family to get in serious trouble?

"Everdil?" Mama called. Her footsteps padded down the hallway. I can't explain why, but I covered "Emmett's head" with the sheet.

I closed his door, practically shaking as I held my finger to my lips like a librarian when I faced Mama. "He's still sleeping." The lie slipped out so easily it was like the difficult decision had been made subconsciously for me.

"Oh," she said, fully believing me. "Breakfast is ready."

Mama had mixed up some oatmeal with brown sugar, golden raisins, and a touch of milk. Even the most basic things she cooked taste amazing.

"You haven't seen my new blender or my mixing bowls or where the bag of flour went, have you, Everdil?"

I shook my head no, feeling a pulse of pain in my tooth. I took the sensation as a good sign that the nerves were working properly.

"I must be losing my mind," Mama said as she rinsed the oatmeal pan. "I suppose I need to organize a few things."

"Definitely," I said, maybe a little too enthusiastically.

Mama stopped what she was doing and sat next to me, looking me right in the eyes. "Your papa and I haven't made some of the best choices. We'd give you and Emmett the world if we could." She sighed. "We're making some changes, and the bank might be willing to work with us."

It was a relief to hear her finally acknowledging the financial trouble instead of pretending like I was ignorant. "I'll help any way that I can. That's a promise."

"I'm counting on it," Mama said, kissing my cheek lightly. "I already have a favor to ask. I don't want to leave you and Emmett alone with all this madness going on in town, but the café is short staffed and apparently busier than it's ever been. Will you two stay out of trouble?"

"We'll see," I said, doing my best to avoid making a promise I couldn't keep.

Mama thought I was making a joke using one of her favorite phrases. "Good one, Everdil. Gramps and your dad will be at the marina, so call them, or call me at the café if you need anything. I'd keep the home phone disconnected unless you need to use it. I'll check in later, regardless."

Mama wrapped me in a hug so tight that her worry seemed to pass through her embrace. If she only knew.

25

Potter's Point seemed like the obvious place where Emmett (and possibly the others) had gone given the discovery of the body, but it had to be crowded with news reporters, researchers, and Bigfoot nuts like Swamp Sam. They would've sent a group of kids home or notified their parents somehow, right?

My mind went back to Swamp Sam. He'd been keeping a low profile after shooting rock salt at Emmett and Tim and the shopping incident. Maybe the team had gone back to investigate the gnarled tree near Swamp Sam's cabin thinking it was a signature mark of Bigfoot. This made the most sense, but the thought of going there alone to check on them was enough to make me break out into a sweat. I had a feeling that Swamp Sam wouldn't take it easy on me because I was a girl or that he'd care about who I was any more than he cared who Emmett and Tim were. My idea was to get in and get out before getting caught.

By the time I got ready, you would've thought I resembled a real hunter. While I didn't have a gun, I stashed a steak knife in my backpack for just in case. Goodness knows Mama had plenty, and she was already missing several things. My backpack was so heavy with supplies: the camera, snacks, and water, that it took me a moment to find my balance on my bike. Even so, it was much easier to ride than Gramps' bike.

While visitors came to Uncertain, our little town had never been so crowded as I biked to Swamp Sam's cabin. The inns and bed and breakfasts had flipped on their "no vacancy" signs. The Uncertain Café had a line of customers that snaked out the front door and along the side of the building. Some of the folks were dressed up in suits and dresses with high heels like they might've been news reporters, while others wore grubby clothes and camouflage vests. Mama had to be slammed preparing food for all those folks. She'd hopefully make some good money.

I maneuvered the bike down an alley to be less noticeable, but I nearly flipped off when I rammed into a recycling bin. *Crunch!*

So much for being less noticeable—an oversized shepherd-mix charged me, growling as it nipped at my bike tires.

"Be a good puppy," I said, baby-talk like. This did nothing to disarm the dog.

I pedaled to a shortcut that led out of the alley. Like the boar had, the shepherd gained on me, snapping at my backside.

I zoomed onto the main street where a BMW nearly splattered me.

The driver held up his hand in aggravation, and I'm sure he would've flipped me the bird if he hadn't been missing his middle finger. The man sped off, but not before I got a good look at his George Washington-like features. Dierk Robinson had nearly killed me.

Another car turned around the bend, but I was paying attention this time and so was this driver. The dog had enough sense to get out of the street, and I took this opportunity to zoom off.

Swamp Sam's cabin was deep in the woods, so I rode my bike as far as I could along dirt paths and tire tracks. When I got closer in, I left the bike near a broken windmill to sneak around more stealthily on foot. After what happened to Emmett and Tim, plus to Tim's bike, I figured this was safer. If you could call it that.

Nothing around here seemed out of place—no ripped pieces of yellow shirts, bedazzled clothing, or shaggy brown tufts of hair were caught on the brush. I searched for messages like "help" carved on the trees, not like I was expecting anything so extreme or so obvious. Really, it was just your typical hot Texas summer day in the middle of nowhere East Texas.

With the backpack weighing on my shoulders, I took a short break and chugged an entire water bottle and gobbled down a granola bar. When I continued on, the weeds were taller and thicker, making it hard to see any trails or tire paths. I pulled out my compass to head northeast taking shelter under the shade of large oaks when possible. If my sweat was any indication, it had to be over one-hundred degrees.

This was a waste of time. I should've learned my lesson that day I'd explored alone in the woods. Why hadn't I involved the sheriff and Mama and Papa? I had to be about the dumbest twelve-year-old in all of Uncertain. In all of Texas. In all of—you get the point.

As I was about to give up, a shotgun blasted. Birds squawked and scattered from the oak branches. This was close. Too close.

Swamp Sam could've been shooting at Emmett and the others ... if they were even here. I wish I could say I rushed into a dangerous situation Chuck Norris style for a chance to save them, but I stood in place, trembling as I debated about what to do.

My tooth injury had been painful enough, and I couldn't imagine how awful it would be to get shot, especially with a real bullet and not just rock salt. I told myself this wouldn't happen, and that if my days had already been numbered, well then that had been determined long ago.

This wasn't the most comforting of thoughts, but it was enough to propel me forward, taking shelter near the trunks of the oaks for more than just their shade now.

My stomach already churned from the images running through my mind, but I about lost everything I'd just downed when I caught a whiff of something horrid. Like a rotten container of pot roast long forgotten in the fridge sort of horrid.

I anticipated another shotgun blast, but it was eerily quiet.

Even the birds seemed to be holding their breath.

As much as I wanted to leave, I couldn't. Not until I could somehow check that Emmett, Tim, and Shawna weren't here. After a few minutes and an intensifying stench in the air, I spotted the tree Tim had mentioned before, bent exactly like the one on Goat Island. While this tree wasn't as enormous, it was just as unusually mangled. I stayed hidden here to scope out the area. Other than this mysteriously bent tree, there weren't as many other trees or hiding places around.

Off in the distance, I spotted Swamp Sam's cabin, which was cluttered with massive piles of junk—a tractor, some metal bins, oversized burlap bags, and things I couldn't quite make out. It had been several years since I'd gone with Mama to deliver a meal to Swamp Sam after he'd been hospitalized, and I couldn't recall the place looking this run down. What stood out the most at the time were the multiple mounted game heads decorating the interior staring at me with their vacant glassy eyes.

Behind the cabin was a work area that I could barely see from here. About ten feet away from it stood a pile of something reddish-brown. Of all the supplies I could've used right then was a pair of binoculars, but Shawna was the one who owned them. I snapped a photo and used the zoom feature to try to get a better look. The pile appeared almost blood-like, but the viewing screen was too small to see much detail.

A light breeze rustled the leaves on the bent tree. You would've thought I'd been shot at the way I jumped from how much it startled me. The breeze also carried with it an intense wave of foulness. The deer poaching scene flashed in my mind, and I couldn't wait to get out of there. I told myself that I could leave as soon as I confirmed what the pile was or wasn't.

I accepted my fate no matter what, but it still took me a few moments before I gathered enough nerve to leave the protection of the bent tree. I stretched the way Emmett did before a football game. He'd be brave right now if he was here. Tim would mastermind some kind of plan, and Shawna would march right up to Swamp Sam and smooth talk information from him.

I did what I could, bending down to crawl in the clearing. Chuck Norris would've been to the East Coast by now, but crawling took me a lot of effort. My arms were like soggy spaghetti noodles from the intense effort of propelling myself forward. The backpack had to go. I laid flat on my belly and chugged more water before I abandoned my supplies. The only thing I kept was the camera plus the knife, which I tucked in my sock military-like, careful not to cut myself.

This was a precaution I hoped would seem silly. I left the backpack near some type of shrub with little purple flowers, positive I'd be back in a few minutes to retrieve it.

26

Once I got within twenty feet of the cabin, I took cover behind a rusted Oldsmobile. The car hadn't gone anywhere in years—tall weeds weaved their way through the tire rims. Stench haunted the area like an angry ghost.

The wood stain on the cabin had faded, and several of the boards were warped, not like I was paying that much attention to the cabin with so much clutter around, plus the pile. The nauseating pile. Now that I was closer, I confirmed that it was indeed blood. Right as I identified body parts—hooves, antlers maybe some intestines—there was a flurry of motion. I ducked down by the Oldsmobile's passenger door. As soon as my shaky legs were steady enough, I squatted to get a better look.

Beyond the pile, resting against a scrappy looking loblolly

pine was Bigfoot! His body was slumped, and he wasn't as large as what I'd seen before. I snapped a photo and then another, stopping when Swamp Sam approached Bigfoot. He was armed with a shovel.

I almost yelled out for him to be careful but then watched as he took the shovel and dumped something into Bigfoot's body. Using the camera's preview screen, I zoomed in and saw that this was no real creature—just an ape costume. One that was in the process of being stuffed with guts. It reminded me of a sausage making show I watched on FoodieLand, only you know, much, much more disgusting.

Oh man. This had to mean that what Papa and Dierk had found in the pit was likely a hoax like this one.

Between the rotting body parts and this realization, I couldn't control it any longer. The car groaned as I leaned my body against it for support as I wretched. I hadn't intended to be so loud, but try throwing up silently. You'll see it's next to impossible.

My stomach wasn't relieved after. No, not when I heard footsteps. The sound of boots clomping on the ground grew louder.

I had two options. Run or stay put.

Emmett, the notorious running back, hadn't been quick enough to avoid getting shot at. Staying put seemed more reasonable though hardly at all.

"Who's there?" Swamp Sam said, his voice hoarse.

Like I planned on answering.

There could've been snakes and who knows what else hiding

in the weeds beneath the Oldsmobile, but I backed my way under, legs first. I should've been eating more fruits and vegetables instead of Emmett's treats because it was a tight squeeze. And itchy.

I stopped when my necklace caught on something.

The footsteps grew closer. "I said who's there?" Swamp Sam's voice sounded menacing.

I pulled at the necklace to unhook it, but the chain was too caught up. The necklace dug deep into my skin.

Gramps had trusted me with this heirloom and so had Mama—it was priceless. But I valued my life more.

I yanked my neck so hard that the necklace nearly cut off my air supply before the chain snapped off. The pearl dropped into the patch of grass right in front of me.

Just as I almost grasped it between my fingers, a hand wrapped around my arm. My yell had to ring out louder than the shotgun blast.

Swamp Sam drug me out from underneath the car, his grip so tight I couldn't reach for the knife in my sock. I really don't know what I would've done had I been able to grab it. I hope you know I'm not the type of person who would've stabbed someone. Especially considering I was sneaking around on his property in the first place.

"Another nosy spy, huh? Since when did the agency recruit children?" Swamp Sam's pupils were huge, and his face peeled even more.

"Nobody sent me. I'm looking for my brother and his friends."

"I'm sure the government trained you to say that. Bigfoot turned on me, and Raleigh's kids got infiltrated," Swamp Sam said and mumbled a few incoherent things about booby traps and conspiracies.

If the situation hadn't been so dire, his nonsense would've been funny. "I promise we don't work for any government agency," I said. "We just want to win the Bigfoot contest. Do you know anything about it? A million dollars for a picture—"

Swamp Sam ripped the camera from me. "Tell me exactly who you work for and why you're after me!"

"Nobody. We want to win the contest, honest. My family could use the money—you know how Papa recently took over your marina—"

"You don't know what you're messing with. The beasts have begun stalking humanity, and the government is training them for an uprising. I'm doing my best to threaten them."

Whoa. Swamp Sam was even sicker than I'd realized. I closed my eyes and prayed I wouldn't end up chopped up as part of the gruesome-ape-costume-stuffing-mix. I thought of a Chuck Norris fact to distract him. "If there's ever an apocalypse, hang out with Chuck Norris because he won't worry about surviving. The zombies will."

Well, that was a failure. Swamp Sam was done talking and dragged me to who knows where.

"Please don't hurt me!" I dug my feet into the ground.

Swamp Sam kicked at my legs and picked me up.

"I won't tell anyone what I saw if you let me go."

"You've transmitted too much data already."

"That's not even possible." He was carrying me to a hog trap that had to be at least eight feet long. It's too embarrassing to share how much begging I did to change his mind. I can't even bring myself to repeat it.

"Silence," Swamp Sam said.

I struggled to keep him from tossing me into the cage, but he overpowered me when I reached for the knife. I'm not sure if I would've stabbed him or not at this point. With my arm extended, he wrangled and shoved me inside.

I threw my body forward and attempted to claw my way through the door. Swamp Sam slammed the cage door on my hand. I reeled back in pain, clutching my fingers. He clicked the latch into place and secured it with a lock. "I refuse to get manipulated. Transmit that," he said, scratching at his neck and mumbling something about a ransom.

Trouble doesn't describe the situation. Doomed is more like it. Not only was the cage locked up like a jail cell, I couldn't move my middle finger.

"No more problems from you," Swamp Sam said. He inspected my camera for a moment like he considered keeping it for himself, but then he tossed it to the ground and stomped on it with his boot several times. I watched until the camera was nothing more than bits of shattered technology. Then he left me there trapped like a helpless animal.

I had no idea what his intentions were, and I didn't want to stay in the trap long enough to find out. He'd already been busted with criminal misconduct with a weapon in the past.

As soon as Swamp Sam was out of sight, I reached through the bars to unclasp the gate. The lock didn't budge. I tried to use the knife to pick the lock, but I couldn't get a solid enough grasp. My middle finger was now misshapen and had begun to swell. Good thing it had gone mostly numb.

After another attempt, I dropped the knife to the ground. NO! It fell a few feet outside of the cage.

I knelt down to try to retrieve it. My broken finger knocked it even further away. I couldn't lose the only thing that offered any protection. I reached with my left hand this time instead, so far so that my armpit pinched against the metal. I could finally touch the blade and pull it in, slicing my skin in the process.

Blood trickled from my left index finger after. Great. Just great. I used the bottom of my t-shirt to wrap my finger, though it took more effort than you could imagine. I'm sure the risk of infection was high, but that had to be the least of my concerns.

I sank to the floor, sitting on the ground, just now noticing a corn trough at the other end of the cage. The rotted smell in the air was strong from here, and the cage had an odor that was a mixture of urine and fear from whatever had been trapped in here before. Like I was now.

An hour passed or maybe it was only a few minutes—already I felt like I was losing my mind like Swamp Sam had. Besides getting myself trapped, I still didn't have any answers regarding Tim, Shawna, and Emmett.

I needed that life rewind button more than ever. I dwelled on how I should've told them goodbye.

I should've told Shawna that even if she wasn't my friend anymore, she'd been a good one in the past. We'd both messed up.

I should've told my brother he annoyed me, but I couldn't imagine life without him.

I should've told Tim I liked him instead of just hoping he realized it.

This Should've Game didn't do anything to help this mess, so I came up with some unlikely ingredients for future episodes of Garbage Can Gourmet.

Fish oil.

Lime rinds.

Stale potato chips.

Apple cores.

Can of olives.

Overripe banana.

Cayenne pepper.

Leftover barbecue.

Frostbitten steak.

Pigs feet.

Deer antlers.

Well, that brought me back to reality.

I threw my whole body around, hoping the trap would collapse so I'd be free. Just like the lock, it didn't give the slightest. The only thing capable of escaping was a stream of tears.

27

Gram once said that the tears from Chuck Norris could cure all diseases … if only he'd ever cry. I pulled myself together. I was thirsty enough as it was and had a huge headache. The numbness in my hand had started to morph into searing pain, but I refused to give up.

I went back to trying to unhook the latch. The knife was too wide. Time was hard to gauge, but based on the position of the sun, it had to be well after noon by this point. I was drenched in sweat so I rested my hand and my whole body, too. When I did, I found a gap in the earth underneath the weight of the heavy metal bar of the cage. I could use the knife like a shovel and dig my way out. Or die trying.

I couldn't think like that. Chuck Norris could beat the sun in a staring contest, and he'd find a way to get out this situation.

I stabbed the knife into the ground. The blade wobbled from the firmness of the dirt—this area must've missed the recent storm. Because of my injured hands, I held the handle awkwardly and scooped at the dirt instead. The earth gave some, but only about a tablespoon at a time. It would take forever before I'd be able to dig a hole large enough to crawl out of.

I froze completely when a loud screech echoed through the area. I could almost see a towering dark shadow behind a tree.

Swamp Sam was approaching the cage. He glanced around like he wondered where the ape-like noise had come from, too. "Stop watching me!" he shouted at the woods. He'd changed into a pair of cleaner jeans and white shirt with a blood stain on the shoulder. He carried something. A container, maybe.

I stood over the area I'd been digging to hide it. When Swamp Sam reached the cage, he was holding a plastic half-gallon jug of milk filled up with a clear liquid. It didn't have a cap on it.

"Here," Swamp Sam said, squeezing the container through the bars. Some of the liquid dribbled out, splashing my feet. I almost backed up and revealed the hole I'd dug under the cage. He grunted and jiggled the container at me.

I hesitated before taking it from him. It could've been full of poison to make me fall asleep before he hacked me up to bits. Or it could've just been regular old water. I planned on waiting until later to inspect the liquid further before deciding whether or not I'd drink it. If I stayed locked up long enough, I'd have to. And even with my front tooth in bad shape, the corn in the trough might have to become snack fodder. Chuck Norris wouldn't need to eat. He'd find a way to gobble up fear.

I must've said this out loud because Swamp Sam asked, "Is this Chuck Norris person in on the plan?"

I laughed. "I wish."

Swamp Sam scowled. "No funny business until I figure out what to do with you." He glanced at my hand, which had swelled up even more, scowling at the sight of it. Maybe I just imagined it, but it seemed like a wave of concern or worry washed over him. His shoulders sagged, and he took a slow, deep breath. Without another word, he trekked back to the area where the stuffed costume had been. He struggled to carry it off.

A few minutes later, a brown pickup truck pulled out from behind the cabin. It was hard to see from the vantage of the cage, but I was sure that had been the same truck I'd observed that gruesome day in the woods. As I'd found out today, Dierk drove a BMW, and there was no doubt at all that Swamp Sam had been the poacher. Now I knew what he was up to.

I should've made the connection sooner. I really had to survive this to let everyone know what was going on.

Once the sounds of the truck disappeared into the distance, I sniffed the liquid. It didn't have any odor, but given the disgusting smells in and around the cage, maybe my nose couldn't be trusted. I wanted to believe that Papa's old boss wouldn't poison me, but he was mentally ill and had already broken my finger and locked me away.

Between the cut on my left hand and the broken middle finger on my right, it didn't matter whether or not I planned on drinking the liquid because I dropped the entire container as I brought it away from my nose. I stepped back, and it hit the ground with a thud, the contents glugging entirely out.

At first, I thought that was the drop of death. People died from dehydration for crying out loud! Then I saw how much darker the earth had become right where I'd been digging.

Mud! Mud would make digging easier.

And it did, though "easy" doesn't describe how much effort it still took to create a hole large enough that I could slip my hand through to the other side.

The process seemed to take hours, but I couldn't be sure because some dark clouds had moved in, blocking the position of the sun. I prayed for rain.

While that went unanswered, at least the shade protected my skin from frying to a crisp. When my neck and shoulders ached too much to scoop out another speck of dirt, I took a break and scanned the area again to keep watch for Swamp Sam's return. So far, the truck seemed to be long gone.

When the hole was only several inches wider and deeper after all that effort, I almost gave up. I shook so much that I had to lean against the cage to steady myself. My throat was dry—so dry— but I sung to keep myself from wondering what Chuck Norris fact Emmett was going to share at my funeral.

Right as I got to singing about "boots made for walking" again, another unidentified screech rang out. This time it sounded more song-like, as if it were in-tune in a primate sort of way. Or at least how I imagined a primate would sound. I looked across the field but didn't see anything but a few trees and grass as far as the eye could see.

I repeated the line, and there was another songful wail. Bigfoot. It had to be. Maybe it was a stretch, but the creature seemed to be comforting me. And I was certain the scream I'd heard a short while before had been a warning about Swamp Sam approaching. Who knows what would've happened if he'd caught me trying to escape. And the day I got lost in the woods? Those sounds could've easily been Bigfoot guiding me to safety.

Swamp Sam's conspiracy theory about Bigfoot was way off, but I'd been misguided, too. The creatures seemed harmless and intelligent even if they were large and had especially menacing fangs.

I reflected on Mr. Nash's story of his miraculous rescue. I'm not going to lie—I had a few doubts before, but I fully believed now.

Maybe Shawna hadn't been lying about seeing a baby Bigfoot. It wasn't out of the realm of possibility—there had to be family units to carry on the species, and while it seemed almost impossible to actually see one, I felt certain about my own sightings.

As I sat there, trapped and feeling hopeless and hopeful all at once, I reached the conclusion that some things couldn't be explained. Perhaps they're not supposed to be.

I'd stopped singing, but Bigfoot cried out a mournful tune that flowed right through to my soul.

The thought of such a mysterious creature being mangled and tortured and who knows what else people like Dierk Robinson and Swamp Sam would do—well, I couldn't take it after the awful things I'd witnessed.

"Get away from here before you get trapped, too!"

I leaned back to rest, but the dark shadow from behind the tree approached. My vision was blurry from a combination of exhaustion, dehydration, and cloud coverage, but there was no doubt what I was seeing. The long black-brown fur. The incredible stature.

Not what I was seeing. Who I was seeing.

Bigfoot.

My idea of the family units had been correct. This Bigfoot was a she—the animal had a bulky chest like the nursing female gorilla I'd seen at the Houston zoo.

Her mouth was closed or else the fangs would've freaked me out even more in that moment. Bigfoot's eyes were filled with soulfulness as she inspected me. They rendered me speechless.

This moment was so surreal that it's almost a blur. I don't

remember saying anything or doing anything, but I felt a sense of peace as she grasped the bars of the cage.

Just as she was about to bend the bars enough to free me, the ground rumbled.

A vehicle was approaching.

Dear God, protect me. Had Swamp Sam returned already?

Bigfoot fled the scene with remarkable agility given her size. I didn't thank her. Maybe I wouldn't live long enough to get the chance.

I turned my head to the side to try to squeeze my shoulders through the bars, the dirt mashing into my face. Inhaling dirt will make you sneeze no matter how quiet you're trying to be. That's a fact I can certify.

Despite the pain, I clawed at the ground to push the rest of the way through. The hole wasn't large enough at this point. I was stuck.

A door slammed. My body was so wedged between the metal bar of the cage and the ground that I couldn't back my way under, not quickly enough before Swamp Sam would catch me.

All I needed was a few more minutes. A few more minutes I didn't have.

This was it.

The end of Everdil Lynn Jackson.

28

I closed my eyes, replaying the scene with Bigfoot in my mind instead of facing the fact that I was about to be discovered by a crazy man. Maybe Bigfoot would come back and get me out of the cage.

The woods were silent again. No birds chirping, no knocks, no wails, no singing. Just my heart crashing against my ribcage.

"Everdil?" a voice called. It sounded like Gramps.

My face was so close to the ground that my mouth filled with grit as I yelled, "Here! I'm over here!"

I nearly broke my neck trying to see who was approaching. Things were still blurry, but I identified Gramps' favorite flannel.

I heard my name called several more times, and I kept yelling, "Here!"

"Everdil!" Emmett said, rushing over to the cage. He sure could run fast.

My chest was so squished that it was difficult to talk, but the fight wasn't out of me. Not a chance. "Help me get out of here. You'll never believe what just happened."

Gramps and Emmett weren't alone. From this angle, I watched as Shawna's wedged sandals and Tim's unlaced boots approached.

They inspected the slightly bent bar as I told them what happened. "You scared her off."

My family and friends looked around suspiciously and fussed over me. Shawna squatted down close, holding her half-finished water bottle up to my parched mouth. I would've forgiven her for just about anything for this act of kindness. Even after chugging the rest of the water, my throat still felt dry and scratchy. "Thanks, and I'm sorry—"

"If anyone is sorry, it's me. I wish I could take back what I said. Take back a lot of things, really."

Tim's voice cracked as he said, "Me too." He knelt down and reached for my hand. I almost pulled it back to protect my mangled middle finger, but it's not like I could go anywhere. Tim must've noticed the injury because he placed his palm softly on the back of my hand.

My ribcage ached, partly because of being trapped and also because my heart still hadn't calmed down. Tim's gesture didn't help any. Emmett and Shawna and Gramps were all watching him, but he kept his hand in place. He leaned down even more, until his forehead rested against mine. He was so gentle about it that I didn't have to worry about him cracking my skull or knocking out other teeth.

Tim said nothing, yet it seemed like the best conversation we'd ever had. Unlike the hand incident before, this was clearly no accident.

Leave it to Emmett to ruin the moment. "I'm a rotten big brother," he said. I thought he was going to get sappy on me, but he didn't. "Who do you think you are, Everdil Pickle Breath? Chuck Norris? Did you take Swamp Sam's 'no trespassing' as a dare?"

"Think fast, Emmett," I said, my voice barely above a whisper. "Tuna can oil, cayenne pepper, an apple core, and pigs feet."

"No clue," he said as he scraped the ground to get me out. "You finally got me."

Once Tim let go of my hand, he dug furiously. Like an army on a mission, Emmett, Gramps, and Shawna attacked the ground. Not only did I want to escape for the obvious reasons, I had yet another reason: to try and win the contest. We needed the money, of course, but I wanted to raise awareness. I understood Mr. Nash's motivation to protect Bigfoot on a deeper level. If they'd survived all these generations living on the fringes of humanity, they deserved to continue doing so.

"I knew something was wrong when you weren't home," Emmett said, stirring up a small dust cloud that made me choke. My brother slowed down, digging more carefully as he continued talking. "I thought you might've gone to the marina, so we went there to look for you, and that's when we ran into Swamp Sam talking about Bigfoot spying on him and how he was holding an agent captive and that the area had another surprise in store. Dierk Robinson told Papa he saw you biking this direction—"

"I bet Dierk didn't say about how he almost ran me over. I was trying to find *you*, Emmett," I said, keeping out the part about him sneaking out. It was trivial at this point.

"That's what I figured. After the three of us checked out Potter's Point last night, we saw how many people were arriving. I got an idea. The contest might've been over, but the chance to make money wasn't. After gathering some items, we stayed up the entire night baking Bigfoot cookies at Tim's while his dad was gone—"

Shawna cut Emmett off. "Tim designed several foot-shaped cutouts, Emmett made the dough, and I decorated the cookies."

Tim dug with the intensity of a terrier, but I wanted him to stop and hold my hand again. "We made over four-hundred cookies," he said, practically out of breath.

"And we made a killing on them. Mama let us sell them at the café for a dollar a piece, and we sold out by noon."

I wondered if Mama realized that's where her missing items ended up. The closer I was to escaping the cage, the more it hit me that the team had been baking cookies while I'd risked my life to find them. Baking cookies! "I thought you all were still hunting for Bigfoot and had been chopped up to bits." I shared how I'd gone looking for them here because of the tree clue and then discovered the pile of guts. I *really* should've learned my lesson the first time. "The Bigfoot Papa and Dierk Robinson found has to be a hoax," I said, filling them in on the rest of what I'd witnessed and how Swamp Sam caught and trapped me.

"That's what the experts discovered, Everdil, and now we know who did it. Sam will pay for this," Gramps said. "Sorry it took so long for us to get here."

"I had it covered with Bigfoot's help," I said, untwisting my shoulders and working the rest of my body through. What had taken me so long to accomplish before took much less effort with help. I could've done it on my own, though. No doubt.

"That's my Everdil Pickle," Gramps said and laughed despite the circumstances.

It was like my soul had been inflated with helium, and I laughed too as I made it out of the hog trap. I'm not going to lie—pain roundhouse kicked me from my teeth to my fingers to my toes, but I was alive and free. So very, very alive and free. The whole group gathered around me, cheering and helping me to my feet.

Across the clearing, a tree shook the way a cheerleader might wiggle a pompom after a touchdown at a football game. "Check that out," I said, pointing and listening to a loud *Whoop!*

"Well, I'll be," Gramps said. The rest of my teammates stood there with curious expressions.

"Bigfoot's celebrating, too," I said and shared more about my experience. I'm sure I sounded a little like Swamp Sam as I told them how Bigfoot approached the cage and what she looked like.

"Bigfoot needs to be protected, not hunted."

"I believe that's why I couldn't kill the one I saw when I had the chance," Gramps said.

Before I could leave the area, I inspected the scraps of my camera. It was several boot stomps past the point of repair, but I dug through the parts until I found the memory card. I slipped it in my pocket, hoping the pictures could be salvaged somehow. And then I saw something that blew my mind. The pearl nestled in the camera debris.

"How did it get here? I lost it over by the abandoned car."

"Bigfoot could've hand delivered it to you," Shawna said. "I wonder if she's the mother of the baby I saw?"

Neither was past the point of possibility. Nothing seemed past that point anymore.

Gramps had been lucky to find the pearl the first time, and it seemed even luckier the way I mysteriously found it the second. I still can't explain how it got there to this day.

"Let's get you to the hospital," Gramps said. My legs wobbled as we walked to the VW Bug.

Having just spent time at the dentist office, the last thing I wanted to do was head to a hospital, but if I wanted to keep my finger and not have some awful infection from the cut, I knew I had to go. I should never have poked fun at Dierk's finger.

Shawna gagged when we passed what remained of the pile of guts. Emmett put his arm around her until the color came back into her face, and then he kicked a bag of rock salt that was on the ground.

Gramps shook his head in disbelief. "I had no idea Swamp Sam was so off his rocker."

I held my injured hands up in the air to minimize the throb that happened with each step I took. Would Tim have reached for my hands again had they been okay?

When I stopped obsessing over wanting him to, my delusional mind went back to the pearl and the soulfulness of Bigfoot's eyes. My voice was less scratchy when I said, "We should refocus Team Bigfoot." I shared how I wanted to do what I could to protect the animals and conserve their habitat.

"We could give a portion of the proceeds from our cookies. I can make up other Bigfoot-related recipes," Emmett said, reminding me of Mama when she got excited about one of her auditions.

The rest of my team was willing to shake on this, but well, they had to settle for a light fist bump with my left hand.

29

"Everdil sits shotgun," Emmett insisted. Gramps helped buckle me in.

I nearly passed out from the comfort of the car seat and the exhaustion from the experience as Gramps drove to the emergency room in Marshall.

"I've been giving this a lot of thought," Shawna said. "Tea bags, chicken fat, candy canes, and prunes."

"I got this one!" Tim said, intercepting Emmett. "Roasted chicken with a nasty, chunky mint sauce."

"I'd eat it," Gramps said, smiling. "Prunes are good for an old man like me."

The Ingredients Game stopped as soon as Shawna's phone got coverage. First, she called the police, telling them about how

202

Swamp Sam had trapped me after I discovered that he'd been mutilating animals and stuffing costumes. Either the connection was bad or the police didn't believe her because she repeated herself a couple of times. She kept the part about Bigfoot helping me out of the conversation.

Emmett borrowed the phone from her afterwards and called both Mama and Papa to fill them in. I was fading in and out but could tell he wasn't giving them the full version of what had happened which was probably for the best because they were going to flip out.

"They'll meet us at the emergency room," he told me after he passed the phone to Tim.

Tim updated his dad on the situation. "Yes, sir, I'm sorry for the mess. Yes, sir, I understand."

After Tim hung up, he handed the phone over to Shawna. "I'm grounded for the next week for the mess we left in the kitchen," he said. Given how junky their house was, I'm surprised his dad cared so much, but rules were rules. I for one was done breaking so many of them.

That wasn't the end of the many phone calls. Shawna rang her dad and talked to him for what seemed like a while trying to help Papa out with some of the legal trouble between him and Dierk. "Your dad should be able to get paid for what he deserves and maybe even more," Shawna said after hanging up. "Dad said he's looking forward to me coming home at the end of the summer, but I'm not sure what to do. Mom and my grandma need me, and

I'm not sure if Dallas is my home."

Emmett and Tim pleaded for her to return to Uncertain, and Shawna watched me carefully for a reaction as if she wanted my blessing or something. "You have to do what's right for you and your family, but I hope you stay." I wasn't lying. We were all imperfect stooges, and I hoped we could return to normal, even if it was a new normal between all of us. "Thanks for trying to help out Papa," I added. Shawna and I had a lot more to talk about, but it would have to wait until I recovered. Tim, too, for that matter.

The trip to the emergency room is nothing more than blips of memories, especially after I was taken back and the nurses hooked me up to an IV and the doctor ordered some pain meds. You're not supposed to have many people with you at the emergency room, but the staff made an exception for my friends and family since they considered me a celebrity. I do remember telling the story about what happened several times—to my parents, the hospital workers, and to some police officers that arrived, and to one reporter.

Even Mr. Nash showed up at the hospital, and when he saw Tim, he said, "I'm proud of you." The way he looked at Tim reminded me of the picture in Mr. Nash's office, only Tim was the one now dwarfing his dad. That and he didn't wear a monkey costume these days.

Other reporters requested to talk to me, but Mama insisted I needed my rest. She was right, and it probably wasn't long before I drooled a big old puddle in front of everyone. I can't be sure because Emmett never gave me a hard time about it.

Shortly after the ER trip, the sheriff found Swamp Sam at a drug store buying a first aid kit after he'd planted the second costume around Old Stagecoach Road. I'd like to think he was buying the first aid kit to help me fix my finger. Regardless, he'll be spending a lot of time in the slammer. I hope he gets the help he needs. By the way, he denied digging the pits. Just like the pearl, no one is really sure what to think about it. Only Chuck Norris could find the answer. Chuck Norris could stand at the bottom of a bottomless pit if he wanted to.

With the contest going strong again, I felt compelled to write everything down that happened, which hasn't been easy for me. Team Bigfoot helped out some, though we've renamed ourselves the Team Bigfoot Bakers.

It turns out that frosting cookies is good physical therapy for hand injuries. Plus it's kind of fun. Shawna says it's like giving flour a makeover. Anyway, I'm much better at using decorating tips than throwing them. We plan on designing some custom aprons, but for now, the boys and Shawna are rocking the cupcake aprons. They let me wear Mama's boss apron. Mama says I'm quite the pastry artist.

Business is good for Team Bigfoot Bakers, and twenty percent of the cookie proceeds go to a conservation fund that Mr. Nash started. He's planning on presenting it at the fall Bigfoot conference. Shawna used her smooth talking skills, and now a few local shops carry our cookies besides the Uncertain Café. Emmett's just about ready to launch a Bigfoot lollipop complete with chocolate Bigfoot "hairs." Mama's gotten a whole bunch of catering offers, and the touring business is going well for Papa and Gramps.

A new necklace chain should be arriving in the mail soon. Mama made an exception about ordering it from a TV infomercial so I could wear the lucky pearl again. When Gramps first gave me Gram's necklace, he said something about feeling rich despite the circumstances. He didn't think I understood what he meant, but I can say with certainty that I do.

Dear Cryptic Cryptid Productions,

P.S. — I'm sending you my story, of course, but I wanted to share a few other things. Shawna's dad is making business cards for Team Bigfoot Bakers using the picture of the four of us I've included. It's obvious, I know, but I'm the girl wearing the torquoise dress. Shawna is the one with the burgundy streaked hair, and you can sort out the boys based on their height differences. We wanted to share some cookies, too. Hope you like them!

Tim recovered the pictures from the camera's memory card, and I've enclosed this as well to give you as much evidence as I'm able to provide. I do realize that the photos and videos are lower quality than what you're looing for and don't scientifically prove Bigfoot's existence, but I hope you think my story matters.

Regardless of what happens, thanks for reading and considering this entry. Please don't forget to call!

Love,
    Everdil Jackson

cryptic
cryptid
PRODUCTIONS

Dear Ms. Everdil Jackson,

Thank you for your submission and thank you for your patience. We have been overwhelmed with entries for the Cryptic Cryptid Contest, and unfortunately, no winner has been selected for this calendar year though we will be pursuing claims for future episodes on our show.

Uncertain, Texas and Raleigh's Tours seem like locations worthy of investigation to raise awareness. Please know that we read your story with great interest—so much so that we've forwarded your story to an editor in our mass media corporation's publishing division.

Best of luck and keep up your important mission!

The Producers

Cryptic Cryptid Productions

P.S. We've sent word to our sister network, FoodieLand, to be on the lookout for an audition from chef enthusiast, Macy Jackson and her sous chef son.

ACKNOWLEDGMENTS

The phrase "it takes a village" certainly applies to this book, and I'm indebted to so many wonderful folks for making this story happen. To the all-around amazing P.J. Hoover, I don't know where this story would be without you or where I would be. Thanks to Tara Creel, E. Kristin Anderson, Kendra Friel, and Christine and Katie Marciniak for the helpful feedback. Andrea Cascardi, thanks for shaping the story and giving me the right push I needed. I'm grateful to Erszi Deak and Georgia McBride for their part in this book's journey. My Lodge of Death fellow writing retreaters will always have a special place in my heart as will the Austin writing and book community in addition to the Hollins children's literature community. Thanks for the book love, Margie Longoria, Kelly Milner Halls, and P.J. Hoover!

I respect and admire you so much, Madeline Smoot! Thanks for giving this book a chance and for your hope and enthusiasm. I love that our friendship has spanned a couple of states and a couple of decades. It has been such an honor to work with you and Jeff Crosby. Jeff, your art is absolutely stunning, and I'm so incredibly honored that you said yes to illustrating the cover and the interior!

Thanks to everyone at the Uncertain General Store & Grill for sharing stories and providing inspiration. Much appreciation goes out to the Texas Bigfoot Research Conservancy (now known as North American Wood Ape Conservancy) for helping me research Bigfoot.

My family is wonderful beyond words! At the time I began drafting this novel, my mother was fighting for her life. She has overcome so many difficulties—her strength, generosity, and determination continually motivate me. My father's love and strong work ethic also serve as a wonderful source of motivation. I could say similar things about my wonderful in-laws. Thanks for being so generous and supportive, Glen and Alfrieda! Zachary, Jill, Grant, and Seth—you all inspire me in more ways than you will ever know.

Thank you to the nth for being such a wonderful sounding board and advocate, Michael. You are a wonderful husband, and I will always be thankful for your advice, encouragement, plus your enthusiasm for things like taking a long road trip to Uncertain, Texas to help me research and imagine where Bigfoot might've wandered. Ava, you were just a dream in my heart when I first started this project. Thank you for constantly showing me that anything is possible.

While there isn't enough space to thank everyone individually since this book took so many years to get right and to get in print, please know I'm incredibly appreciative. If I won a million dollar Bigfoot contest, I would want to reward you all for your love, patience, and kindness!

ABOUT THE AUTHOR

Jessica Lee Anderson loves to write, and she enjoys imagining the possibility of the impossible. She is the author of *Trudy, Border Crossing*, as well as *Calli*. She's published multiple chapter books for Rourke Educational Media to include such titles as *Brownies with Benjamin Franklin, Case of Foul Play on a School Day*, and *Runaway Robot*. She's published fiction and nonfiction with Heinemann, Pearson, Seedling Publications, Six Red Marbles, and a variety of magazines including *Highlights for Children*. Jessica graduated from Hollins University with a Master of Arts in Children's Literature, and previously instructed at the Institute of Children's Literature and St. Edward's University. She is a member of The Texas Sweethearts & Scoundrels and hopes to be more sweetheart than scoundrel. She lives near Austin, Texas with her husband, daughter, and two crazy dogs.

Visit www.jessicaleeanderson.com to learn more.